ALL TIED UP

A Deadline Cozy Mystery - Book 3

SONIA PARIN

D1366598

ISBN: 1539113833

ISBN-13: 978-1539113836

Chapter One

"CAPTAIN JACK BLACKTHORN... everything a man should be... Magnificent build. Easy, playful manner. Oozing sex appeal..." Eve rolled her eyes, "I don't like this one bit." All these women daydreaming... entertaining fantasies about her man.

"Did you say something?"

Eve looked up from the stack of letters she'd been reading. Mira's fan mail. Eve had now been living in Rock-Maine Island with her aunt for several months. Needing something to do, she'd been helping Mira with some of her author housekeeping duties... "I'm having trouble dealing with this surge of interest in Jack."

Mira laughed. "He's become a favorite with my readers."

Detective Jack Bradford had come into their lives a few months before when he'd been investigating a murder on the island. They'd now been dating for a few months.

Mira, a.k.a. historical romance author, Elizabeth Lloyd, had been so inspired by Jack, she'd fashioned her latest swashbuckling hero on him. And while Eve had at first been amused, now she wasn't so sure she could share Jack with Mira's enthusiastic reading audience. The thought of all those women curling up in the evenings and filling their fantasies with him was putting her on edge. "What if your readers find out he's real?"

"But he's not," Mira reasoned.

"You said you based Jack Blackthorn on my Jack." Eve had now read Mira's, or rather, Elizabeth Lloyd's latest historical romance three times and with each reading Jack Blackthorn had become bigger than life.

A couple of days before, she'd been on a date with Detective Jack Bradford and had surprised herself by wondering why Jack couldn't be more like... Captain Jack Blackthorn.

Eve tilted her head and smiled as she recalled one particular chapter from *The Princess and the Sea Wolf.* Captain Jack Blackthorn had launched himself from the highest ship's mast, and had swooped through an ensuing battle to land on another ship where he'd swept the reluctant damsel—

"Eve."

"Sorry, did you say something?"

"Perhaps you should give the fan mail a rest."

Eve shook her head. "I want to do something, I need to do something." Until recently, she'd owned a bustling business. Selling her restaurant had left her floundering. She'd never had so much free time on her hands. If she didn't set her mind and heart on something soon, she'd go stir crazy.

"Have you given any more thought to running the bookstore? Or maybe you should just focus on relaxing. This is meant to be your time to redefine yourself."

"I'm not sure I can still use that excuse." She sighed and sunk back in her chair. "I feel I've been going against the current, turning my back on what I know best. It's time I accept my fate. I'm a natural born chef, so I should stick to what comes easy to me. Jill suggested I open a bed and breakfast or an inn. The island gets enough tourist traffic to make it worth my while."

"Then you should look into it. Abby's place is still up for grabs and it's large enough to convert into an inn."

Eve gazed out the window at the sea beyond. Like Mira's beach house, Abby's house sat right by the shore with easy access to the beach. "That reminds me, I need to drop by Abby's place. I promised I'd keep an eye on it." Abby Larkin had recently sold her bookstore to Mira and had packed up to move to the city in search of her happy-ever-after. Instead of keeping the house as a safety net, she'd put it on the market, but so far, she hadn't had any takers.

Eve suspected Abby's asking price had been set too high on purpose. While Abby insisted she wanted to cut all her ties to the island as a way of making sure she stuck to her purpose, she might still be harboring some reservations.

"I might actually do that this afternoon. Is there anything you need me to pick up for you in town?" Eve asked.

"If you happen to be near the bakery, I wouldn't mind some of their chocolate chip cookies. Of course, I prefer yours but I feel guilty neglecting local businesses."

"They do well enough from Jill and me." Not a day went by when she and the twenty-four year old artist she'd befriended when she'd come to the island didn't drop in for a coffee at one of the establishments in town.

Eve nibbled the edge of her lip. She hadn't baked in days. What had come over her? She loved cooking for Mira and she knew for a fact, Mira preferred her cookies. "Okay, I'll finish these letters for you tonight."

"Are you sure? I don't want you to do something that makes you feel uncomfortable."

"Have some faith in me. I can deal with a little jealousy. Besides, at the end of the day I have the real Jack."

"All right, but please keep in mind these are my

loyal readers and they know when someone is being tongue in cheek."

"I promise they won't know it's me answering their mail and not you. By the way, some of your readers want to know if there'll be a sequel to *The Princess and the Sea Wolf*."

Mira smiled. "I'm thinking Captain Jack Blackthorn will put in a few cameo appearances. In fact, I've decided to give him a twin brother."

Eve buried her face in her hands. Great. Now there were going to be two Jack wannabes to contend with.

———

During the drive to Abby's beach house, it suddenly occurred to Eve that Mira's loyal readers were the least of her concerns. Mira had created Captain Jack Blackthorn and that meant she'd spent a considerable amount of time thinking about the real Jack.

Eve tapped her fingers on the steering wheel and tried to remember how Mira had described the pirate.

... broad shoulders, long, lean frame... ruffled brown hair... a playful smile that promised a world of delicious fun...

Her mind meandered to the steamy chapters she'd read several times over. Mira didn't shy away from explicit scenes. Eve fanned herself. The heat level in her books had astonished her. She'd never thought of Mira in those terms...

While they enjoyed an open, friendly relationship, with no holds barred, Eve preferred to nudge the door shut on some matters, never talking about her personal life, something she knew Mira found amusing, if not odd.

Reading those intimate scenes had definitely made her cheeks flush. Some passages she'd read over, snickering like a schoolgirl, and if pushed for the truth, she had pictured herself and Jack... dressed in period costume...

Never mind that the heroine was blonde with a curvaceous figure, the complete opposite to Eve who, despite her healthy appetite, remained slim. She'd once considered changing her hair color but had decided once a brunette, always a brunette. Still, it didn't stop her from daydreaming...

It made her wonder how Jack felt about role-playing.

It made her wonder if he'd read Mira's books...

Should she suggest it?

Seeing a couple edging toward the road, Eve slowed down. Walking tracks crisscrossed the island with locals and tourists making use of them. She'd never before been much of a walker but since moving here, she'd taken up the exercise, mostly as a way of filling up her time. However, she hadn't ventured out too far. Something she could rectify.

With a nod, she decided walking would be a good way to clear her head and find some inspiration. She had plenty to think about. She'd given herself enough relaxing time. Now she needed to push for more firm decisions and sketch out some clear plans.

It would keep her busy, and effectively take her mind off all those women thinking about Jack and using him for who knew what...

As she drove by, the couple waved. She didn't recognize them but she still waved back. She'd been coming to the island since she'd been a little girl, but she'd never thought of herself as an islander. However, for the past few months she had been trying to fit in by building relationships with some of the locals.

Jill Saunders, the twenty-four year old local artist who lived near Mira's beach house, was a constant companion. They often went on walks with Jill's two Labradors, Mischief and Mr. Magoo. And Eve was, slowly but surely, getting to know other people through Mira.

This was all new to her. Having lived most of her life in New York where she'd rarely had more than a passing acquaintance with her neighbors, she'd decided she actually liked the feeling of belonging and of maybe becoming part of the community.

She was about to turn into the road leading to

Abby's house when a sports car pulled out forcing her to break hard.

"Ever heard of giving way to oncoming traffic," she called out.

With her heart thumping all the way up to her throat, she watched the car speed off in the opposite direction and disappear into the distance.

Eve couldn't remember ever seeing it around. Then again, there were over two thousand inhabitants, with plenty of people driving in from the mainland either to visit someone or just to spend the day.

Scooping in a calming breath, she drove the short distance to Abby's place. She'd have a quick look around, and make sure everything was as it should be. The local realtor could be trusted to lock up, but it didn't hurt to check.

She took a few minutes to walk around the property, checking windows and doors. While Abby's house was closer to town than Mira's place, Abby had told her this was the quiet end of the island with most of the surrounding houses owned by people who lived on the mainland.

As she strode in, she gave more thought to the idea of turning the house into an inn. The wide hallway entrance had a welcoming feel to it. Inside, the house looked as if it might have come out of the pages of an interior design magazine. A set of double doors opened to a sitting room with a fireplace. The dining room was on the opposite side of the hallway, with a door leading to a large country style kitchen in the rear with another sitting room attached to it, and a spacious sunroom to the side.

Eve thought it had been a smart move to list it fully furnished. While Jill had removed the more personal items such as photos, there were plenty of decorative items to make the place looked lived in and inviting.

Although, she wasn't so sure about the rifle hanging over the fireplace.

She checked more windows and then made her way upstairs. Not that she thought she really needed to. If anyone broke in, there'd be signs of disturbance downstairs. But she'd become a little intrigued.

Could she really turn the place into an inn?

There were plenty of bedrooms. Another set of stairs led up to the top floor with two more bedrooms, both with uninterrupted views of the ocean. Abby had been using one of them. She'd offered the house with the lot, so the room was still furnished and that was probably why she was asking for so much since most of the furnishings were antiques.

Eve sent her gaze skating around the bedroom. Her attention caught on something glinting next the bedside table.

Too big to be a bracelet, she thought.

Taking a closer look, she frowned.

A handcuff?

It looked real enough.

What would Abby be doing with...

Her mouth gaped open.

Abby.

Naughty Abby.

Who would have thought?

Smiling, she opened the top drawer to put it away and found its twin.

"Well, well. Never judge a book by its cover." Abby Larkin didn't strike her as the type to walk on the wild side. It only went to show one never knew what went on behind closed doors.

With a small shake of her head, she locked up and made her way into town to pick up some cookies for Mira.

Later that evening, she caved into temptation and called Abby to tease her.

"What are you talking about?" Abby asked.

"Pleading innocence, are you? Nudge, nudge. Wink, wink. I can keep a secret."

"Do I look like the type to play kinky games?"

"Well... no. But is there a type?"

Abby growled into the phone. "Could you please do me a favor? Go back tomorrow and get them out of there. I'm having palpitations. What if the realtor finds them? What will she think of me?"

Eve laughed. "It could be a selling point."

"It's a large house targeted at families. Please, Eve—"

"All right, I won't taunt you... much."

They spoke for a bit longer, although Abby didn't have any tales to tell, her efforts to find Mr. Right so far yielding nothing.

"By the way, I just finished reading *The Princess and the Sea Wolf*. All I can say is... hot, hot, hot."

Eve groaned. "Not you too."

Chapter Two

"WHAT'S GOING ON?" Eve asked when she met Jill the next morning at the Chin Wag Café. "It looks like the locals are picketing the place. I had to fight my way past a mob to get in."

"This corner gets the most foot traffic during the day," Jill said, "A few of the locals are up in arms about speeding cars. They want speed cameras installed."

"Where?"

"Everywhere. Did you sign the petition? Linda Brennan organized it."

"I didn't realize there was one." Eve looked out the window and saw a woman holding a clipboard. "Who's Linda?"

"She's the one in the red sweater. She holds the record for the most distance walked on the island. Three hours every day."

Eve glanced at her and thought she looked familiar. "And who's the woman holding the clipboard?"

"That's her walking buddy. Steffi Grant."

"I don't see many people signing up."

"I doubt anyone will. It's a waste of time. I've never seen anyone speeding."

Eve was about to say she hadn't either when she remembered the black sports car that had nearly ran into her the day before. "Do you know anyone who drives a black sports car?"

"What model?"

Eve shrugged. "No idea. It looked expensive. Then again, all sports cars look expensive to me."

Jill shook her head. "Doesn't ring a bell. Most people around here drive SUVs or pickup trucks."

Maybe it had been someone driving in to look at Abby's place. Eve picked up the menu only to set it down again. "Before I order, there's something I need to know."

"You sound serious. What's up?"

"Have you read *The Princess and the Sea Wolf*?"

Jill put her hand to her forehead and swooned. "Oh, Jack. Jack. Jack."

"All right. I get the picture."

Jill grinned. "I usually wait a few months to reread a favorite book but as soon as I read the last page, I had to flip over and start again. Mira's onto a winner with this one. I couldn't really pick a favorite from all her other books, they're all good, but this one is special. There's just something about a pirate—"

"Enough already."

"What? Why?"

Eve made a point of looking around the café.

"Oh, I get it. You're not comfortable with people picturing Jack that way." Jill laughed. "Don't be greedy. You have the real Jack. The best we can hope for is a bit of fantasy."

"You're the most level headed young woman I know and you've lost your head over a fictional character—"

"Based on a real life one," Jill said.

"You should be ashamed of yourself. He's taken."

"I can't believe this. You're really jealous."

"I feel as if I'm being cheated on."

"But Jack hasn't done anything wrong."

"It's going to get worse. Mira's giving Captain Jack Blackthorn a twin brother and he's bound to be another heartthrob. If my Jack finds out, I'll never hear the end of it."

"I didn't realize you were so insecure."

"More like possessive. I don't like all these women... you included, thinking about my man. I know it's silly, but everyone's being so blatant about it."

"Everyone?"

"I'm doing Mira's fan mail. You wouldn't believe how fanatical her fans can be. Imagine if someone finds out about Jack. He could be stalked. And that's not so farfetched. I don't know how the cover artist managed to capture his likeness."

"Mira must have described him."

"Only too well. Now it's too late. I can't ask her to change him."

"Well, if that's your biggest concern, then you can consider yourself a lucky woman. We have to live vicariously. At least you get to play with the real Jack."

Only when he wasn't involved in a case. She took comfort in knowing he'd just wrapped one up, so she had some fun to look forward to.

When the waitress came over, Eve checked the time and placed her order for coffee.

"What? No cake?"

"I need to get going. I promised Abby I'd swing by her place and pick up... Never mind." She should have collected the handcuffs first thing that morning, in case the realtor had an early morning showing but Jill had called to ask if they could meet in town for a coffee as they hadn't seen each other in a few days.

"You can't do that," Jill complained.

"What?"

"Cut me off like that. Now I'm curious. What do you have to pick up?" Jill bobbed her eyebrows up and down. "Abby's secret stash of... naughty DVDs?"

"What made you say that?" Eve asked.

"I don't know, maybe all this talk about fantasizing about fictional heroes." Jill shrugged. "Was I right?"

"No... Not really."

"Oh, that's interesting. Was I close?"

"I promised I wouldn't say anything." She hadn't promised but it didn't sound like something Abby would want everyone to know about. "How's your painting going?"

"All right. I'll find out soon enough." Jill sat up. "I'm between pictures. Do you think Jack would consider sitting for me?"

"You wouldn't."

"Why not? I could make a killing selling paintings of him dressed up at Captain Jack Blackthorn."

Eve gave an impatient shake of her head and changed the subject. "Remind me to grab some chocolate chip cookies for Mira. I tried to get some yesterday but they'd run out."

"You're out of luck. Jonathan McNeil, the baker, is away on vacation."

"What? Since when?"

"Since last week. The other baker's bread is good, but his cookies are fairly average."

"Why didn't you say something before?"

"I had no idea. You normally do all the baking for Mira."

Eve sighed. "I'm off my game. I don't know what's come over me. I think I'm putting too much pressure on myself to find something to do and I can't even focus on the simplest tasks."

"Well, you're going to have to snap out of it. Mira needs her cookies and we need her to be happy and write her books."

"We?"

"Her adoring fans."

Eve rolled her eyes. "Come on, drink up."

"What? Am I tagging along?"

"Yes, please. I can always do with the company."

After making a detour to buy some ingredients for baking, they arrived at Abby's beach house.

"I've never been inside," Jill said. "It's huge."

"She inherited it from an unmarried relative. I think that's what made her so determined to find herself a husband before it's too late."

"Selling this place is a bit extreme. In her place, I'd hold on to it as a weekend getaway."

"Abby's afraid if she has a place to come back to, she'll be tempted to give up her search for Mr. Right." Personally, she would have struggled to let the house go. The house felt comfortable, homey. Inviting. "I won't be long." She dashed up the two sets of stairs and headed toward the main bedroom. As she turned the doorknob, a thought flickered in her mind.

If the handcuffs didn't belong to Abby, then her unmarried relative must have had a few tales to tell. Just because someone wasn't married didn't mean they didn't play around. Then she decided the handcuffs looked too new to have belonged to Abby's aunt.

Pushing the door open, Eve came to an emergency break stop.

Before her brain could engage and shoot out an order, her legs turned to noodles and wobbled.

Her fingers held on tight around the doorknob even as her instinct told her to let go and run.

In the next few seconds she tried to get her throat to work so she could call out to Jill, but it took the last of her willpower to draw in a breath.

It made her head swoon.

With her heart beating an erratic drumbeat against her chest, she managed to get her feet moving into an awkward retreat.

She couldn't tear her eyes away from the bed. Even when she bumped against the balustrade and nearly lost her footing, she continued to look.

She stood there, eyes wide, her breathing coming in short choppy bursts.

A part of her knew she should take a closer look.

Common sense told her she had to.

She shot her gaze down the stairs but before she could change her mind, she pushed off the balustrade and propelled herself back inside the bedroom.

Gritting her back teeth, she pushed out a soft groan. She could do this. She had to.

When she reached the foot of the bed, she scooped in a big breath.

Two more steps, Eve.

The man lying on the bed looked fast asleep, in an eternal sort of way. Fixing her attention on his chest, she waited several seconds, hoping... praying to see the steady rise and fall that would have her running for the right reasons.

If given the choice, she would have preferred the embarrassment of walking in on someone luxuriating in the aftermath of a thorough lovemaking session.

Instead, she'd stumbled upon a lifeless body.

There didn't seem to be any doubt about it now or any point in denying it.

"You're only saying that because you know what comes next." She cleared her throat. "Go on. You can do it." She had to be absolutely certain. She had to feel for a pulse. "On the count of three." She drew in a breath and hissed it out. "One—" Eve plunged forward and pressed two fingers to the side of the man's throat. "Neat trick," she said through clenched teeth.

After only a couple of seconds she snatched her hand away.

He felt cold.

"There's no coming back from that."

Reaching into her back pocket, she retrieved her cell. Her hand shook as she keyed in the emergency number.

"Yes. Police. Yes. Dead. Body." She nodded in response to the operator's request for more information. "Pulse. Yes, I checked. No. No pulse. Address?" She didn't know the address. "Abby's place." As the words spilled out she realized how ludicrous she must have sounded. "Cove Lane. My white SUV's parked outside. Alone? No, I'm not, but Jill can't see this. Who's Jill?" She shook her head. "Just get here. Fast."

She stood there a moment, swaying and concentrating on breathing.

Her mind cranked up and began to process the scene she'd walked into.

Bits and pieces fell into place, like a jigsaw puzzle.

The man's hands were handcuffed to the bed post.

His hair looked slightly ruffled but still retained that styled look she knew cost a small fortune to achieve.

He had a toned build. She guessed he worked out.

At first, she thought his eyes were closed, but now she realized they were at half-mast, as if he'd been gazing down.

Eve drew in a small breath, inhaling through her nose and that's when she picked up the flowery scent. Had it been there the day before? She owned a couple of scents that always lingered in the air and on her clothes.

The strangest thought crossed her mind.

One decision had been taken care of.

She wouldn't be opening up an inn here.

"Eve? Do I need to come up and get you?" Jill called out.

What?

No. No. Jill. Don't.

Her lips were moving, but she didn't hear herself speak.

She moved, one small step at a time, retreating without taking her eyes off the man.

"This place is great," Jill chirped, "You should buy it."

She heard Jill's footsteps coming up the stairs. "No, Jill. Don't. Don't." Eve swung away and forced her legs to move. They responded to her command but the rest of her body remained stiff.

"Hey. What's up?" Jill asked as she reached the top of the stairs. "And what's with the robot walk?"

Eve shook her head. "Nothing," she squeaked.

"You look pale and what's wrong with your shoulders? They're level with your ears." Jill gasped. "Let me guess, I wasn't wrong about the DVDs. Did you find something else? A secret stash of dominatrix underwear? A blow up dolly? I watched a documentary about them. They look so real now..."

"What?"

"I want to see too."

Jill tried to move past her but Eve stretched her arms out like an ice hockey goalie blocking a shot.

"You can't go in there."

"Why not?"

"It's bad. It's very bad in there."

"What do you mean?"

The sound of approaching police sirens had Jill turning toward the door.

"Who's in that bedroom, Eve?"

Eve shifted. "No-one." And that was the truth.

Chapter Three

"I DON'T OFTEN FIND myself in this type of situation," Eve said under her breath thinking that if she said it often enough, she might come to believe it.

She tried to find a comfortable spot on the chair she'd been asked to sit in while the police went about their business, but she felt on edge. Jumpy.

Why wasn't someone asking her questions? And where was Jack?

She knew the moment he stepped through the front door he would be Detective Jack Bradford, and not the man she had intimate dates with. And when his gaze connected with hers, she'd have a split second to capture the hint of amusement she loved about his bright blue eyes. After that, she knew Jack would withdraw. Freeze her out. Distance himself without necessarily leaving her in the lurch. She understood he needed to remain impartial. His job would always come first...

His personal attachments would be set aside.

She knew she could trust his judgment.

A few months before, he'd had ample reasons to come down hard on her. Being the prime suspect in a murder investigation, all fingers had been pointed at her and she hadn't really had a leg to stand on.

Yes, his job came first but that meant he would trawl through all the evidence, putting together a rock solid case. Detective Jack Bradford did not jump to conclusions.

Jill sat opposite her with her feet tucked under her, her arms hugging her chest. Her gaze had remained fixed on a spot somewhere on the floor.

Eve had already checked to see what there could be to hold her interest but she hadn't noted anything interesting about the floorboards or the rug.

"How are you holding up?" she asked.

Jill shrugged. "All right, I suppose." She looked over her shoulder toward the hallway. "How long do we have to sit here for?"

"Your guess is as good as mine."

"They've been up there for a while now."

Eve nodded. "Collecting evidence." Had she missed Jack's entrance? She didn't think so. Whenever he came near her, her body went into alert.

Jill leaned forward. "Should we... maybe... get our stories straight?"

"What's there to get straight? We came together, so we're each other's alibi."

"Alibi?" Jill's face tightened. "I didn't realize we needed an alibi. I just came along for the ride and... Okay, I wanted to see Abby's secret stash of X-rated DVDs."

"I told you there aren't any. I don't know where you got that idea from—"

Jill gave a brisk shake of her head and nudged it in the direction of the hallway. "Police," she mimed.

Eve shifted and saw the police officer standing by the door. Experience had taught her to be careful what she said in front of people because anything she said could be misconstrued and tied in to the...

Murder.

Again? How could this be? When had the island become the centre of criminal activity?

The front door opened.

Eve tugged at a stray lock of hair. Her heart gave a little skip. Excitement bloomed inside her.

Jack.

She heard his long exhalation first. A sigh that spoke volumes.

Yes, she'd once again crash landed right in the thick of it.

"Hello, Eve. Jill."

Curling her fingers around the armrests, Eve slid to the edge of her seat. "Jack."

He motioned for her to remain seated.

She nodded. Yes, she would do as told and co-operate fully. "What brings you here?"

Jack's eyebrows lifted. "You need to ask?" He strode over to her, his gaze skating around her face. "Are you all right?"

"Sure, why wouldn't I be?" Silly question. At the rate she was going, she'd become a veteran witness in no time.

She glanced over his shoulder and saw Detective Mason Lars stride by. At least now she knew how this would play out. Jack would be present during her questioning, but he wouldn't be directly involved. That task would fall on Detective Mason Lars.

He glanced her way and nodded.

It said a lot when a local detective acknowledged your presence.

Jack joined him. Eve supposed they needed to run through their standard tactics, just to be sure.

She hoped she remembered everything that had happened. She hadn't been thinking about it. In fact, she'd tried her best to erase most of it from her mind.

"You should talk to Jill first." Put her out of her misery, Eve thought making a point of checking her watch. They hadn't been waiting that long, but she couldn't see any reason why they should be forced to remain here longer than they had to.

Jack motioned for her to follow. They strode over to the dining room and then through to the kitchen where Jack drew out a chair for her.

Detective Mason Lars cleared his throat.

Knowing the drill, she asked, "From the top?"

"From the moment you arrived," Mason Lars said.

"I opened the bedroom door and found a naked man on the bed with his hands cuffed to the bed post." The fact she cut to the chase without mentioning being at the café and only ordering coffee before coming to Abby's place said a lot about her state of mind. She wanted this to be over and done with. She wanted to go home and bake cookies and think about swashbuckling heroes. Anything to take her mind off the dead man lying on the bed with his hands cuffed...

"Can you tell us what you were doing here?"

"I promised Abby Larkin I'd keep an eye out for the place. She owns the house, but she's selling it."

The detective wrote something on his notepad.

"She doesn't live here," Eve continued, "Abby's already moved to the city. But I doubt she'll be able to help you."

"What makes you think that?"

"She doesn't live on the island. She moved away—" She stopped. If she said any more, she'd have to explain the reasons why Abby had moved and she didn't want to betray her friend's inability to find a boyfriend on the island. Eve decided that, in her place, it wasn't something she would want spread around.

"She's not the type to get into any sort of trouble," Eve added. Then again, that would give her the perfect cover. "She had nothing to do with this. If she'd been on the island, we would have known." Eve chuckled. "I can't imagine her sneaking back in the dead of night in a rowboat." Eve tapped her chin and wondered how long it took for a body to start feeling cold. He must have been killed in the dead of night.

"How often have you been checking on the house?"

"About once a week."

"So you last came here last week."

Eve shifted in her chair. It didn't go unnoticed.

Mason Lars held her gaze for long moments. Eve looked up at Jack who stood nearby and then back to Mason Lars. While Jack's broad shoulders narrowed down to slim hips, Mason Lars's thick neck defined the rest of his body. Solid. Stocky.

"Actually... I dropped by yesterday. I've been thinking about going into business and turning the place into an inn—" She frowned and wondered why she'd told them that. Nerves?

"Yesterday," Mason Lars prompted her.

"Yes."

Eve sent her mind wandering because anything was better than thinking about the man upstairs.

If she wanted to turn this house into an inn, the kitchen could easily be upgraded with a new stove...

She'd have to add a new workbench.

She wondered what else she'd have to do to bring the kitchen up to standard, at the same time Eve prayed the detective wouldn't ask why she'd returned so soon.

"Why did you come back so soon?"

"Pardon?"

The detective exchanged a look with Jack. Eve had seen him doing it a few times before as if pleading with him to rein in his girlfriend.

"Two visits in one week. You must have had a reason."

She brushed her hand across her wrist. "Well... I... I thought I'd lost something... A bracelet." She wasn't under oath, so strictly speaking she hadn't lied. Details, Eve reminded herself, made for a convincing cover-up. What sort of bracelet would she wear? Should she describe it?

She noticed Jack uncrossed his arms and slipped his hands inside his pockets. Was he trying to remember if he'd ever seen Eve wearing a bracelet?

She'd have some explaining to do, if not now then later.

Eve nibbled the edge of her lip. She didn't want to put Jack on the spot. If he had to choose between her and abiding by his code of ethics, she knew he'd do his duty.

Mason Lars nodded. "That'll be all for today, Ms. Lloyd."

Her lips parted, mostly in surprise. "Is that all you want to know?"

"You didn't know the victim and you've never seen him before."

She nodded.

"Then that's all for today."

Eve made a beeline for her car, Jill trailing behind her. She pressed her cell to her ear. "Abby. It's Eve. I'm afraid I have some unexpected... bad news for you." Eve climbed into her SUV and sat back and gave her friend the heads-up. "The police will no doubt be in touch with you shortly, but I thought you might want to know and be ready." She drew in a deep breath and filled Abby in on what had happened.

"In my house? A dead body? A naked dead body. But how? Why? I've never done anything to anyone..."

Eve remembered Abby telling her she'd never even incurred a parking infringement or been caught speeding. "If I knew that, I'd be setting myself up as a private investigator and charging huge fees."

"How did they even get in?"

They?

Of course, there had to have been more than one

person otherwise how would the man have ended up handcuffed to the bed post...

"I didn't see any signs of a break-in. Is there anyone else who might have a key?"

"The realtor, of course."

And anyone who worked at the realtor's office.

Eve smacked the side of her head.

No. No. No.

She wasn't going to think about it. And she was definitely not getting involved.

The police would handle the matter. Unfortunately, she'd already played her part by finding the body.

Eve wished she hadn't.

"What about your neighbors? Do you share your house key with them?"

"No point. They only use the houses on weekends. It never felt right or practical to exchange keys."

"How about spare keys? Did you maybe—" Which part of no didn't she get?

Stop right now, Eve.

She had no business snooping around.

"What?"

"Did you maybe have a spare key in the bookstore? You know, in one of the drawers." Eve thought of the young girls working at the *Tinkerbelle's*. Samantha Beckett had worked there for a year and since Mira would remain behind the scene, she'd employed another sales clerk, Aubrey Leeds.

"I did, but I took it with me when I sold the store to Mira. It's the key I gave the realtor. And... And you have my key."

"I'm not sure I like the hesitation in your voice."

"Well, what do I really know about you?" Abby gave a nervous laughter. "Sorry, this is... This is dreadful. A dead body. In my house. Who'll buy it now? I can't think straight. There are so many questions ricocheting inside my head. What do I do? How did they even get in? Is there any damage to the place?"

Eve knew she'd been thorough. The house hadn't been broken into. So, if they hadn't forced their way in...

The key must have come from somewhere... Someone else.

"By the way, I didn't tell them about the handcuffs."

"Oh, that's a relief... Not."

"I didn't think you'd want it to be public knowledge."

"But they're not even mine."

"So you say."

"What do you mean? Don't you believe me?"

"Abby. What proof do you have they're not yours?"

"Doesn't my word count for anything?"

Eve slumped her head back. "Not in a murder investigation."

Eve scanned her ingredients and checked off her mental list. When she'd returned home, Mira had still been inside her writing cave and wasn't likely to emerge anytime soon. She looked up at Jill who sat on a stool watching her. "They didn't ask you anything?"

"For the umpteenth time, no. Why are you surprised? I didn't even get to see the body. You made sure of that."

"You should be thanking me. That's not the sort of mental image you want floating around in your mind."

"Still, there's no need for you to be so protective. I'm not easily shocked."

Eve turned her attention to measuring her ingredients and deciding what sort of nuts she'd put into her cookies.

"Can I help?"

Eve drummed her fingers on the counter. "You could cut up the chocolate." She set her bowl in place and tossed in the butter and sugar. With her sleeves rolled up, she got to work mixing the ingredients to a creamy consistency.

"You obviously didn't recognize him, otherwise you would have said something."

Eve added the vanilla extract to the sugar and butter mix and then one egg at a time, beating thoroughly.

"I guess you're still shaken from the experience."

Eve sighed. "I'd rather not talk about it. I've decided

to stay right out of it this time. Let the police do their job. They don't need me."

"You say that now. I'll expect a call early tomorrow morning."

She folded in the rest of the ingredients. Gave it all a thorough mix and finally added the chopped chocolate and macadamia nuts. With the dough spread into even shapes on a tray, she adjusted the oven temperature and slid the tray in.

Muttering a colorful curse, Eve turned.

"Who could have killed him?"

Chapter Four

AFTER A RESTLESS NIGHT, tossing and turning and swatting at her mental images of a man tied up to the bed, Eve decided to take matters into her own hands.

She strode up to the bakery, her steps purposeful, her gaze fixed on her destination and nothing... no one else.

She'd promised herself she wouldn't even think about the murder and every time she reminded herself, she ended up thinking about it.

Inside the bakery, she asked to speak to the owner.

According to Jill who knew everyone on the island, Barbara Lynch had taken over the business from her father who'd since retired. She'd been an accountant looking for a sea change and had happily settled into the routine of running a busy bakery, mostly as a way to fill in time before she decided on her next career move.

That was precisely what Eve had decided to do that

morning. Frustrated by her indecision to settle on something useful to do, she thought she might offer her services and bake cookies, at least until the baker returned from his vacation. She hoped a job would also keep her mind engaged and away from thoughts of a killer on the island...

Barbara smiled. "And are you qualified?"

"Yes, I ran my own restaurant in New York and," she held up a bag, "I baked these for you to try. They're chocolate chip with macadamia nuts." She rattled off a list of other flavors she could make.

Eve watched as Barbara opened the bag. Within a second, her eyes closed and she hummed.

"Oh yes, it's in the aroma." She nibbled on one and sighed. "Yes. Come on through to my office, we'll work out the details."

Half an hour later, Eve skipped out of the bakery, a smile in place. Finally, she had a purpose. She would start the next day and in her spare time she would follow through on her plans for something bigger and better. An inn or a bed and breakfast began to take shape in her mind. She could see herself doing it.

Checking for traffic before she crossed the road, she saw a car pull up. Jack. Accompanied by Detective Mason Lars. Were they in town to follow up on a lead?

Eve shook her head and turned in the opposite direction only to stop when Jack called out her name.

"Didn't you see me wave?" he asked.

She brushed a strand of hair back and smiled. "Yes... No, I must have been distracted. Hello, Jack."

"Will you be home later today?"

"You sound official."

"We need to ask you a few more questions."

She looked up and down the main street, as if her answer depended on what she saw there. "Well... I'm starting a new job tomorrow, so I'll be doing some running around."

"Job? Where?"

"Right here at the bakery." Her smile widened. "I'll be baking cookies and, you'll be pleased to know, staying right out of trouble." She tagged on that last bit before he had the chance or reason to reprimand her. "And I'm sure I told you everything I know yesterday. I can't imagine what else you might want to ask me."

The edge of Jack's lip kicked up. "If I didn't know better, I'd think you were trying to hide something. But you wouldn't do that."

Would she?

Yes, if she didn't think it would make a difference and telling Jack about finding the handcuffs wouldn't... surely, it wouldn't make a difference.

Then again, it might paint a different picture.

The clandestine meeting, as she had decided to call it, between the murdered man and his hypothetical lover hadn't been a single occurrence. The couple might have been meeting regularly at Abby's house. In which case, they'd have to live nearby, maybe even on the island. And if they lived on the island, they'd have to have a solid reason for meeting in an unoccupied house.

Had they been married?

Married to other people?

"Is there a point to all this?" she asked.

"To what?"

"Harassment. I walked in on a crime scene and I reported it. What else do you want from me?"

He brushed his hand along her arm. "Are you all right, Eve?"

"Well, if you must know, I'm slightly on edge. I didn't sleep well last night. It's not every day I see something so gruesome."

"Do you need to talk about it with someone?"

She shook her head. "I'm not saying I've been scarred for life. It's just not something one can easily shake off. Who would do something like that?"

"That's what we want to find out."

"Do you have any suspects?" she asked.

He lifted an eyebrow.

Of course, if he had any suspects in mind he wouldn't tell her.

Detective Mason Lars strode up to them. "Well?"

Jack shook his head.

The detective sighed and pulled out a plastic evidence bag from his pocket. "Have you seen these before?"

The handcuffs.

"They're handcuffs."

"And when was the last time you saw a pair like these?"

Eve knew when she had her back to the wall. "I saw a pair of handcuffs yesterday on a dead body lying on my friend's bed."

"Could you run through exactly what you did when you walked into the bedroom?"

"We've already covered that."

"Yes, but we might have missed something."

With a nod, she recited the events, stopping only once to check the sequence. "After I called the police, I stepped out of the room and met Jill. We both stood there until the police arrived."

"You felt for a pulse."

She nodded.

"Did you touch anything else?"

"No."

"Are you sure?"

"Yes, I'm positive." She knew she sounded defensive but a few minutes before she'd been happily celebrating her new job and for the first time since the day before, not thinking about dead bodies...

"Would you mind explaining how your fingerprints got on the handcuffs?"

Her fingerprints.

Eve made a mental note to never again touch anything that didn't belong to her.

She saw no point in denying it, but she had no idea how she would explain her omission. It had been a blatant lie. "All right. I found one of the handcuffs on the floor, picked it up and put it in the bedside table drawer." She spoke slowly and hoped that would divert their attention away from the fact she hadn't told them about it the day before.

"When exactly did you find them?"

"T-the day before I called the police."

"Ms. Lloyd, are you trying to protect someone?"

"Yes, but not only because I know she had nothing to do with this but also because... because she didn't want it to become common knowledge. I mean... she didn't know the handcuffs were there. She asked me to remove them—"

"Are you referring to Abby Larkin?"

She nodded.

"If she didn't know about the handcuffs, then why did she ask you to remove them?"

Eve gave an impatient shake of her head. "I called her and told her what I'd found." Eve brushed her hand across her face. "I'm sure she has a perfect alibi. The handcuffs are not hers and she didn't want their existence to become public knowledge. Abby is... she's sensitive. Conservative. Straitlaced. She's looking for a husband. Something like this could ruin her prospects or... or give the wrong impression about her character. Men might get the wrong idea about what she's willing to do..."

"Is there anything else you think we don't need to know, Ms. Lloyd?"

"If I say no will you believe me?" Her credibility suddenly felt shattered. She'd found reason to lie once, she'd find it again. Eve folded her arms. "You must have found other prints."

"We did, but we happen to have yours on file."

So, they had another set of prints belonging to someone with no criminal conviction.

The police had her fingerprints because soon after arriving on the island a dead body had turned up at Mira's house and the murder weapon had been a frying pan Eve had used that day to fry eggs.

The detective put away the plastic evidence bag and pulled out his notebook.

Eve cringed.

"Are you absolutely certain you don't know the victim?"

"Yes, I mean no, I don't know him. And why would you ask me that?" She speared her gaze at Jack. He could verify it. He could say they were together. In theory, that meant she wouldn't look at another man. Did Jack know that? "Have you found the black sports car?"

"What black sports car?"

Realizing she hadn't told them about it, she filled them in. "I'm guessing the driver is connected." Eve gave the detective a lifted eyebrow look. "Will you be following up on it?"

"Ms. Lloyd, if there's any other information you might have decided to withhold but have now changed your mind and realize it might be pertinent to the case, please contact us."

With a nod, they made their way toward the bakery. Eve tried to move on. She searched her bag for her car keys. Pulling them out, she looked over her shoulder to see if the detectives had gone in to the bakery to buy donuts or to talk to the staff, and if so, why would they need to question the staff? What connection—

It's none of your business, Eve.

She strode down to the travel agency to say hello to Helena Flanders but looking through the shop window, she saw her at her desk busy with a customer.

Eve leaned back and looked down the street. She didn't catch sight of the detectives and their car was still there. She supposed that meant they were questioning the staff at the bakery. Wondering if they planned on making the rounds of all the shops in town, she dropped into the Chin Wag Café. She was in luck, the owner, Cynthia Walker, was behind the counter.

She greeted Eve with a friendly smile.

"I'd like one of your blueberry tarts, please." Eve looked down at a stack of courtesy newspapers on the counter. The murder had made the front-page news in the Rock-Maine Island Gazette but they didn't have much information to report on.

Cynthia placed the tart in a carry bag. "We saw the police cars drive by yesterday. Then someone came in and said they'd gone to Abby's house."

Eve tried to follow the thread of the conversation, or rather, the spread of the vine...

Someone else had then seen the body removed from the house and so news had spread about another murder on the island.

"We couldn't believe something so dreadful could happen at Abby's place. Do you know if they have any suspects yet?"

Cynthia's question didn't strike her as odd. Everyone knew now she was dating Jack. Every other week they had dinner right here on the island and it never took long for word to spread.

"It's not the sort of information that would come up." Besides, now that Jack was involved in the investigation she wouldn't be seeing him until it was all wrapped up.

"We've been playing a guessing game," Cynthia said, "Did the realtor find the body? Or did one of the walkers notice something suspicious?"

Eve considered not saying anything about her involvement but then decided it wouldn't look good once word got out that she'd been the one to find the body, as it was bound to do. She put her hand up. "It was me."

"I suppose you can't talk about it. The newspaper report only said a body had been found. One of the waitresses lives out that way but she didn't see anything."

She noticed voices were lowered and a few people looked over their shoulders or stilled in the way one did when trying to eavesdrop on a conversation.

"It's all bound to come out soon enough," Eve said.

Cynthia leaned over the counter. "But what did you see?" she asked, her voice lowered to a loud whisper everyone could hear.

"Not much. I sort of scrambled out of the room and called the police." She couldn't help scanning the café for anyone paying particular attention to what she said.

A man tapped away on his cell. A woman kept flicking her gaze up to her. A couple of women held each other's gazes without speaking—a dead giveaway, Eve thought knowing that was precisely what she'd do if she'd been sitting with Jill. Nothing but normal curiosity and an eagerness to have something to talk about over the dinner table that night.

She paid for her tart and left. On her way to her car, she noticed Jack coming out of the bakery but he didn't go far. Instead, he stood outside and took a call.

In her car, she was about to pull out when she looked over her shoulder and saw him step back inside the bakery.

What could they possibly be looking for there?

Eve tried to remember who else worked at the bakery. Apart from the counter staff, she remembered only ever seeing a couple of bakers. Jonathan McNeil and a younger guy.

It hadn't occurred to ask Barbara Lynch if she'd heard any rumors about the murder.

Eve pushed out an impatient breath. It hadn't occurred because she'd already decided she would stay right out of it. The last time she'd stuck her nose where it clearly didn't belong, she'd ended up having a gun pointed at her... A gun that had been fired.

"Thank you for the reminder," Eve said under her breath and slipped her sunglasses on. When she pulled away she kept her eyes on the road.

And just as well.

Five minutes into her drive, she was cut off by a car turning ahead of her.

A black sports car.

Chapter Five

EVE FOLLOWED the black sports car at a sedate pace. Or at least, she tried to.

"Where do you think you're going?"

It seemed to be increasing the distance between them.

"Where's the trust? We're traveling along the same road... heading in the same direction. I call that coincidence. You must be paranoid if you think I'm following you." As long as she could stay within sight of the car, she wouldn't... shouldn't increase her speed.

Eve frowned. "And exactly what do you think you're doing?" she asked herself.

People were trained to give chase. The police underwent rigorous training in offensive and defensive high-speed driving. Just because she had a driver's license didn't mean she had the experience to follow someone.

When the car disappeared round a bend, she called for patience, but she'd never been the patient type so she increased her speed slightly.

At the last minute, she held on tight to the steering wheel. Her tires screeched. With her back teeth clenching, she leaned into the turn.

"Okay, note to self. Next time, increase speed only after you've gone around the bend."

Straightening, she spotted the car.

It seemed to be further away than it had been.

Shifting in her seat, Eve clenched her teeth.

They were headed away from the bridge, which meant the car belonged to a resident.

But where had it been coming from?

The other end of the island?

Keeping her eyes on the road, she tried to bring up a mental map of the island.

Had the driver been coming from Abby's place?

If so, where were they headed now? She included herself because no amount of common sense would convince her to give up her pursuit now.

"Hang on." She tapped the steering wheel. "I know where we're going."

They were on the road to the marina. At least, she thought they were. She'd never driven along this stretch of road before but she remembered seeing a brochure of the island and the marina had been highlighted with a couple of photos and a small map.

For a moment, she appeared to have lost sight of the car but then Eve realized there was a dip in the road ahead. Within a few seconds the car reappeared.

In the distance, she could see the ocean, which meant they were getting closer to the marina.

She hoped so, otherwise she wouldn't be able to justify following the car. What could she say if she was confronted? She was out for a scenic drive?

Of course, once she got to the marina, she'd have to think up a reason for being there.

Could she play the tourist card?

If she had a road map...

Eve bit the edge of her lip. Had she kept the brochure?

She reached inside her glove compartment.

"Good girl." Grabbing the brochure, she slipped it inside her handbag, a possible scenario unfolding in her mind. If she ended up following the car to the marina, she could get out and pretend to be a tourist. The brochure would give her credibility.

When the marina came in sight, Eve slowed down. She had a perfect view of the sports car and would see it either make a right turn or continue on along the road.

She didn't dare take her eyes off it. Not now that she'd come so far.

"Yes!" She pumped a fist in the air and sat up straighter. The car had driven straight into the marina parking.

Within a couple of minutes, she pulled in and found a parking spot, keeping a discreet distance because at this stage of the game she definitely didn't want to arouse suspicion.

The driver remained inside the car.

Eve couldn't see beyond the tinted windows. If she lingered too long, she risked exposure. So, she emerged from her car and looked around the way someone would if they weren't quite sure of where they were.

"I'm looking one way and now the other and, oh heavens, I'm not sure where I am," she murmured to herself, "I wonder if there's someone around who might be able to help me."

She took a few tentative steps and stopped. This time, she lifted her hand to shield her eyes from the sun.

Because I'm a tourist and I'm lost, she thought.

Seeing the driver's car door open, she stared.

"Just wondering if you'll be the type to help a tourist trying to find her way," she said under her breath, trying to keep herself in character.

Finally, the driver emerged from the car.

A woman.

Dressed in yoga pants and an oversized cable sweater, her honey blonde hair shifted in the light breeze. She ducked back inside the car and brought out a large handbag.

Before she could get away from her, Eve strode

over, not bothering to hide the fact she was intent on catching the driver's attention.

"Excuse me," she called out.

The woman didn't respond, so Eve hurried her steps and called out again.

The woman gave her a cursory glance, took a step and then stopped.

"Yes?"

"Hi. I'm... Laura Boyd." Eve smiled, adjusted her sunglasses and pressed her hand to her chest as if the pace she'd set had been too much for her.

The woman's expression didn't shift. Unfortunately, she didn't provide her name. Eve had known it would be a long shot.

"I hope you can help me. I think I'm lost." She patted her chest, again giving the impression she was trying to catch her breath. "I'm glad I found someone. For a moment there I thought I'd have to drive around the island again."

The woman gave her a faint smile.

"I'm trying to get to the lighthouse."

"Sorry, I can't help you. I'm not from around here."

"Well, do you think there might be someone in the marina who could help me?"

"I'm not sure. You could try the main office," she said pointing toward the pier."

An inspired thought sparked inside her. "If it's not too much trouble, I have a map of sorts." She rummaged through her bag doing her best to sound frustrated. "Sorry, I have a love/hate relationship with my bag. It's the perfect size, but I can never find anything when I want it. And especially not with sunglasses on. Here, would you mind holding them for me?" She didn't wait for a response and instead handed the woman her sunglasses.

From the corner of her eye, Eve could see she was none too pleased, although Eve couldn't decide if this was because she'd stopped her or because she'd asked her to hold the sunglasses.

Taking her time, Eve hunted for her brochure. "Here it is." She looked at it and sighed. "You know what? I know exactly where I am and I think I can find my way now. Sorry for the inconvenience. Oh, and thank you for holding those for me." She took the sunglasses from the woman, careful to hold them by the edges.

Smiling, she tried to commit the woman's face to memory but then decided that would be a waste of time because unlike her aunt, Eve wouldn't know how to describe the woman's features.

Plump, wide lips?

High cheekbones...

Nodding, the woman took off in the direction of the pier.

Eve waited a few moments to see if she went into the office or if she headed to one of the boats.

Belatedly, she remembered her cell. Pulling it out,

she snatched a picture and just for good measure, she took a few of the car.

Back in her car, she set her sunglasses down on the passenger's seat, again taking care to hold them by the edge.

With any luck, the woman might have left a few prints.

Eve had no qualms about tricking the woman. Better to be safe than sorry. Maybe she had a perfectly good reason for driving out of the same street where Abby's house was... on the same day Eve had discovered a dead body.

———

Back in town, Eve spotted Jack's car still parked in the same spot.

"I wonder if you've made as much progress as I have," she murmured as she strode along the main street, looking into the shops. When she saw him and Detective Mason Lars at The Mad Hatter's Teashop, she stopped.

"Okay." She hadn't actually figured out how she'd do this. If she owned up to following the black sports car, she'd get into trouble with Jack. Or he might over-look the fact. After all, she'd saved them a lot of legwork.

Undecided, she sunk down on a bench and waited

for him to come out. Checking her watch, she saw that it was coming up to lunchtime and she hadn't had anything to eat since breakfast.

Half an hour later she'd lost count of the number of times she'd shifted positions. Had they found a reliable witness in the shop? Maybe the owner lived near Abby's house. She made a note to engage her in conversation and find out, right before reminding herself she'd fully intended keeping her nose clean.

Too late now, she thought.

However, once she handed the sunglasses over she would wipe her hands off the whole ordeal.

When she saw Jack coming out of the shop, she surged to her feet.

"Jack." She couldn't read his expression but it didn't matter. Once she told him she was in possession of a set of fingerprints, he'd...

Give her his severest scowl.

"I thought you said you were going to be busy today."

"Yes, but something happened."

"Is this where I have to issue a warning not to go looking for trouble and interfere with the investigation?"

"Strictly speaking, I didn't go looking for trouble."

"It found you?"

She folded her arms. "You should at least wait until you know what I have for you before casting aspersions on my character."

"Sorry, my mistake. What can you help us with?"

"That's more like it, although you could drop the sardonic tone."

"All right. You have my attention."

"Do you have an evidence bag?"

He looked over his shoulder and signaled to Mason Lars. "It looks like we have something to add to our goodie bag," Jack said.

"Follow me, gentleman."

They crossed the street to her car. Eve unlocked the front passenger door and held it open for Jack. "In there. The sunglasses."

Using the plastic evidence bag as a glove, Jack retrieved them.

"Wait a minute. These look like yours."

"Very observant, detective." She smiled. "They are mine and I'd like them back in one piece, please."

"So, what do we have here?"

"Fingerprints belonging to the driver of one unidentified black sports car. A woman, blonde and about a head taller than me. She has a boat moored at the marina."

Jack's eyebrows drew down.

"Oh, and I have some photos." She produced her cell and showed them. "I'm sure your lab people can zoom in on these and get the boat's name." She scooped in a breath. "Oh, and you can run the number plates on her car."

Jack sighed. "Eve."

"Yes?"

"How did you get her fingerprints?"

She wanted to say a good detective never revealed her sources or resourcefulness but she knew that would be asking for trouble. "Female wiles." She gave him an impish smile. "I asked her to hold them for me. She didn't suspect. If she had, I can assure you I would have run a mile."

Eve only then realized the significance of what she'd done. She'd only set out to get a closer look at the driver, but the police could now compare these fingerprints to the ones on the handcuffs and they could also find out if the woman had a record. And, of course, the number plates would give them an identity.

"So," Eve said, "Can I have my fingerprints back now?"

Jack laughed.

"It's only fair."

"That's not the way it works."

She huffed out a breath. "Worth a shot. You'll at least let me know her name, won't you?"

Jack grumbled under his breath.

Her lips parted. "Hey, I deserve some gratitude."

"Yes, of course. Thank you. But next time, it would be better if you called us first."

"By then, the woman might have made her escape.

In fact, what are you still doing here? You should be high tailing it over to the marina."

Detective Mason Lars chuckled and patted Jack on the back. "We better do as the lady says."

Back at Mira's house, Eve couldn't sit still. She still had a pile of fan mail to get through, but her attention kept wandering.

What if the woman was connected to the victim? The police hadn't released a name so she might not even know...

If they were related, surely, she would have reported him missing.

Would have. Should have.

What if she hadn't because his disappearance meant...

She was finally free of him?

Her plan had worked?

There were some people out there prepared to pay for the services of a hired killer and the reasons...

There could be so many.

Eve's marriage had been straightforward, meaning she and Alex hadn't toyed with anything unusual. But Eve wasn't so naive as to think that was the norm. There were couples out there doing all sorts of things. Wife swapping... threesomes...

Eve drummed her fingers on the desk.

"Are my fans causing you grief again, Eve?"

"Mira! You've come back to us."

"First draft is done. Every time I finished a chapter, I would consider stopping for a break but then I'd get a diamond of an idea. Anyhow, I deserve a treat."

"Oh, I have just the thing for you. I picked up a blueberry tart for you today. I'll go put the kettle on."

Eve strode into the kitchen humming to herself. She'd sit down, have a cup of tea, a piece of tart and a chat with Mira. Her head would clear of all this nonsense about extra marital affairs and...

Looking up, Eve yelped.

A face was pressed against the window.

Chapter Six

"JILL. What are you doing here? You nearly gave me a heart attack."

"Sorry."

Jill sounded out of breath and she looked slightly pale. "Are you all right?"

Mischief and Mr. Magoo wagged their tails and pressed their noses against her leg. Eve bent down to give them a scratch behind the ears. "Hang on you two, I have treats for you."

"There's someone out there," Jill said, her breath coming out in little bursts.

"What?"

"Out there. We were coming out onto the clearing when I caught sight of a shadow by the front sitting room window. There was someone looking in. When they heard me coming, they took off."

"Which way?"

"Back out toward the road. I can't be sure, but it looked like a woman."

"Did she have blonde hair?" Eve asked.

"I couldn't tell. It was too dark and I think she had a hat on. But I could tell it was a woman by the way she ran."

"How tall?"

"Taller than you."

The black sports car driving blonde had been taller than her...

"Sit down. I was about to put the kettle on. And there's no way you're going home alone. Stay here the night."

"Shouldn't we call the police?"

"What do you think they'll do?"

"They might be able to intercept the car. She can't have been out on foot."

"Why not? You are. And she'll be long gone by now."

"What's going on?" Mira asked as she came into the kitchen. "Hello, Jill. You're here late."

"Hi... I was..."

Eve motioned for her not to say anything.

"I was out for a walk and... I lost track of time. Yes... I know it's late to be out and about."

"All right," Mira said, her tone distracted, "You two girls have fun. I've been struck by inspiration and it doesn't happen too often. I always have to trawl my way through the proverbial ninety nine percent perspiration, so I should go back in and jot down a few ideas before they fizzle out."

"I'll bring in some tea and a piece of tart for you, Mira." Eve looked at Jill and pressed her finger to her lip.

Jill waited for Mira to leave. "What?"

"Mira's busy writing. We shouldn't worry her with all this nonsense."

After Eve made sure the door to Mira's study had closed, she sat down with Jill and told her how she'd followed the black sports car earlier that day.

"You followed her?"

"I had to. It was like a carrot dangled in front of me. I couldn't resist."

"Next time, take a deep breath and count to ten. And then think of the consequences."

"I'd never get anywhere if I did that." Eve put herself in Blondie's shoes. What would she have done if she'd known someone had trailed after her? "What if the police followed up on it and checked to see if the fingerprints matched and the woman became suspicious. In her place," Eve said, "I would ask how, when, why the police had my fingerprints. Let's pretend I was the only person she had contact with that day. She might have come to the conclusion that I had something to do with alerting the police."

"But you did."

"That's beside the point."

"Yes, but how would she know where to find you?" Jill asked knowing exactly where Eve had been going with her reasoning. "And what did she think she'd do when she came here?"

Eve shot to her feet and went to get a pen and some paper. "Okay. I have another thought. I've seen her driving around the island. Now I'm thinking she suspected her husband... or boyfriend... or lover of having an affair and since I was the only person she had contact with, she thinks I'm the other woman trying to get a close look at my competition. Some women are like that."

Jill's shoulders rose and fell. "That theory is so out there, I think you might be onto something."

"That's what I think too."

"But how did she find you where you live? Even if she connected the dots and realized you'd put the police onto her, how would she know where to look for you?"

"Hang on, I have to take this in to Mira." Eve took a tray into Mira's study. When she returned, she poured them each a cup of tea. "Have some blueberry tart." What would she do if she wanted to find someone and didn't know where to look? "My car. She must have seen me get out of my white SUV. So, she drove around the island looking into people's driveway until she spotted my car. You saw her peering in so she must have been trying to catch sight of me to confirm I was the driver of the white SUV."

Jill shivered. "You seem to have made an enemy. Again."

"Without even trying. I can't even go around minding my own business."

"Were you minding your own business when you followed her?"

"I didn't have a choice. What would you do in my place? She cut me off."

"What did she say when you confronted her about that?"

"I had my priorities, Jill." Eve rolled her eyes. "I seized the moment. Inspiration struck and I realized I could use the opportunity to try to get her fingerprints."

"So now she knows where you live. I'm not feeling very safe."

"Nonsense. We can't be sure it was Blondie. And what can she do?"

"For all we know, she might have been the one to tie up the man and kill him," Jill mused.

"If she had, then why hang around?"

"To kill again." Jill clicked her fingers. "Or it's one of those weird character traits. You know, like people who light fires and then mingle with the crowd of onlookers to watch the chaos. They get a thrill out of it."

"She'd have to be supremely confident to risk

getting caught." Eve pulled out her cell and dialed Jack's number. He picked up on the second ring.

"Are you all right?" he asked.

"That's a strange way to answer a call."

"Not when the call is from you," Jack said.

"I'm not comfortable with you jumping to conclusions, Jack. I could be calling about something else..."

"Such as?"

"I don't know... Well, you know. Something fun, unexpected..."

"What are you wearing?" he asked.

"Yes, that type of call and I'm not saying that's the reason why I'm calling now. Did I catch you at a bad time? Tell me you're not still at work."

"What's this about, Eve?"

"It could be about me wanting to chat with you, but it's not. Still, I don't want you to get into the habit of expecting bad news from me. I'm much nicer than that. Anyway, Jill says she saw someone lurking around outside."

"When?"

"A few minutes ago... about ten minutes ago."

"And it took you that long to find your phone. Oh, wait. Let me guess, you chased after the intruder."

"I did no such thing." Although, it would not have been a first for her. "I was here minding my own business and about to make some tea for Mira. Jill arrived and alerted me. I had to deal with her first. She had a panic attack." Jill rolled her eyes and Eve mouthed an apology. "Also, Mira happened to walk in and I don't want her worrying so I had to wait for her to leave the room. Anyhow, I called you as soon as I could."

"You mean, as soon as you realized you were bound to get caught withholding evidence again." Jack chuckled.

"Be serious. My life could be at risk. I might have acquired a stalker. What if they break into the house in the middle of the night and mistake Mira for me? No one would really care if something happened to me, but... heaven forbid, if something happened to Mira, I'd have to deal with her adoring fans."

"If something happened to you, I'd care."

"Thank you. That's comforting and Jill just gestured that she too would care."

"I'm five minutes away from you. Keep talking. And you don't need me to tell you to stay inside the house."

"You didn't need to come here. How am I going to explain your visit to Mira? I don't want her thinking I'm up to no good." Eve gestured for Jill to close the door leading to the sitting room. "Leave the car out on the road and come in the back way. Oh, and avoid the gravel path. Walk on the grass."

"Any other instructions?"

"Yes. Just because you're a trained detective doesn't mean you shouldn't take care. They might still be out there. What if they hit you over the head and then pretend to be you and come in? You could put us all at risk."

"Have I ever told you what a macabre, twisted imagination you have?"

"Is that a compliment or are you being critical?"

"Your hair looked pretty today."

Eve smiled. "Thank you." She sat down and took a sip of her tea and thought how nice it felt to enjoy a comfortable silence. "I just realized. You're driving and talking on the phone. You're not setting a good example for us civilians."

"Okay, I'm outside your place."

"And you didn't see anyone out on the roads?"

"No."

"Still. You should be careful. They might have hidden the car."

"Does your wildly vivid imagination ever wind down?"

"No, it's highly caffeinated. And just so you know, I'm holding a fire poker."

"Liar."

"All right, I'm sipping my tea. But you shouldn't let your guard down. The last thing I want is to open the door to you and have you collapse into my arms."

"You've been watching late night TV."

"I thought I told you to avoid the gravel."

"I'm still in my car."

"Oh." Eve gestured to Jill and pointed outside. "I can hear someone walking outside."

"I'm on it. Stay put. Do not, whatever you do, leave the house."

In the next few moments, Eve and Jill heard the crunch of hurried footsteps along the gravel path. Then nothing. A second later, another set of footsteps rushed along the gravel path. Jack, she assumed, hot on the heels of the intruder.

Both Eve and Jill had their faces pressed against the window but couldn't see anything. "Mira's study would have the best view. She obviously hasn't heard anything, otherwise she would have come out."

Someone approached the house. Huddling together, Eve and Jill moved toward the back door.

A light knock on the window drew them closer.

"Jack." Eve opened the door to him and threw her arms around him. "What happened? Did you give chase?"

He nodded. "Is everyone okay in here?"

"Yes. But what happened?"

"Just a boy out looking for his dog."

Jill shook her head. "I'm sure the person I saw was a woman."

"We think it might have been the black sports car driver."

"How did you reach that conclusion?" Jack asked.

Eve drew back. "Have you been drinking coffee?"

"Maybe."

"You were out on a stake out." She frowned. "Hey, you were watching this place."

"I was... out and about."

Eve stepped away from him and folded her arms. "What did you find out about the woman? It had to be something bad, otherwise you wouldn't be out here staking the place out."

"I'm not at liberty to say."

"What if I come across her? Should I keep my distance? Call for help? Run for my life?"

"All the above."

"She's dangerous?"

"She's angry."

Eve swung away.

Wife? Girlfriend? Mistress?

"Is the boat hers?"

Jack sighed. "It's actually a yacht, and that's all I'm saying."

She raked her fingers through her hair and gave a firm nod. "That tea's gone cold." She put the kettle on. Turning, she saw Jack disappear into the next room, so she followed him. "Why are you checking the windows?"

"It doesn't hurt to be careful."

"Are you going to organize a squad car to park outside?"

"Even as we speak. You girls should stick together."

Jill huffed out a breath.

"See what you've done now. You've got Jill all worked up."

"You don't need to worry. No one knows of your involvement in the case."

"What do you mean?"

"No one knows you found the body. You should be safe. Just keep to yourself and don't talk to anyone about what you saw."

Well... it might actually be a bit too late for that.

No one knew... No one except the people who'd overheard her tell Cynthia Walker at the Chin Wag Café she'd found the body.

Chapter Seven

EVE LEFT strict instructions for Jill to stay in the house with Mira. Belatedly, she wished she hadn't agreed to start work at the bakery. She considered calling in and getting out of it, but she couldn't bring herself to do it. They'd shaken on it...

As she pulled out onto the road, she gazed at the squad car parked within a discreet distance of Mira's house. She hoped the police realized the house could also be accessed from the beach.

If she had any doubts about the town's grapevine efficiency, she put them all to rest. She didn't even make it half way to the bakery when a local stopped her.

"You poor dear. If I'd found the body, I'd be a nervous wreck. How are you holding up?"

She'd seen the woman around town and now she knew her name. Had Carol been at the Chin Wag Café the day before when Eve had been talking to Cynthia Walker, or had she heard the news through the island grapevine? Eve gathered her handbag close to her and looked over her shoulder.

"I've been too busy to think about it, Carol."

"I can't begin to imagine what it must have been like for you. Was there much blood?"

Eve made a point of checking her watch. "I don't mind telling you, I've never been so scared in my life. I nearly tripped over myself trying to get out of the house." She raised her voice slightly so anyone walking past would hear her. "So, I didn't stop to look at anything. Sorry, I have to run. I don't want to be late on my first day. I'm starting work at the bakery."

Great. Now everyone would know where to find her.

An hour later Eve wondered if there was something wrong with the wall clock. She'd never been so aware of time standing still. She only had two hours of work to get through and she'd been checking up on Jill every fifteen minutes. The sooner she finished her shift and went home, the better she'd feel.

As a customer, she'd never actually noticed the set up in the bakery, which said a lot about her so-called observation skills. Everyone could see her through the glass window. When she'd first started out as a chef, she'd worked in a restaurant where the customers had had full view of the kitchen and she didn't remember ever feeling so self-conscious.

Now...

Every glance told a story.

A scary story.

I'm coming for you.

She tried to distract herself by taking mental snap-shots of everyone she saw coming into the bakery.

"Eve, your cookies are a big hit. I'm taking orders for tomorrow."

She gave Barbara Lynch a distracted nod and tried to catch sight of a customer who kept ducking under the front counter. So far, she managed to identify everyone as locals. Then a new face appeared.

She noticed the woman because she didn't take her sunglasses off.

They were unfashionably large and sat on what Mira would probably describe as a Patrician nose—long and narrow.

Eve pretended to reach down for something. Squatting, she edged away from the window.

"Are you right there?" the baker asked.

She nodded.

Timothy Johnson grinned and squatted down beside her.

"I... I thought I lost an earring."

He looked at her ears. "They're both on. Do you need a hand getting up?"

She grumbled to herself. Timothy couldn't be older than twenty-five. In her thirties, she probably looked ancient to him. "No thanks." She rose but kept her back to the window. "Can you tell me if that woman with the glasses is still looking in?"

"What woman?"

She swung around. Instead of the mystery woman with oversized sunglasses, she stared at the black sports car driver.

Eve had tied her hair back and she wore her chef's white jacket. Would Blondie recognize her from the day before? She didn't appear to be looking straight at her, not in an obvious way, but she was definitely looking. Her gaze skated over the counter. She appeared to be trying to make a selection. When she flicked her attention toward the window, Eve pretended to wipe the counter.

"By the way, your cookies are the best," Timothy said, "I'm trying to figure out what sets them apart."

"*Muscovado* sugar. It has a strong molasses content. It works best with chocolate cookies," she said distractedly. The blonde was now perusing the pie display case. Was she biding her time? Waiting for Eve to leave? No, she wouldn't be so obvious about it. She'd be lurking in a corner, on the opposite side of the street.

Jack had warned her to keep her distance but he hadn't given her any specific reasons other than to say the woman was angry.

Eve decided she must have made the connection

between the sunglasses, the fingerprints and the police showing up at her yacht.

They can't have matched the ones found on the handcuffs. Otherwise, she wouldn't be out and about.

Just how long did it take to make her selection?

She should have made her purchase by now.

Clearly, she was killing time.

Eve drew out her cell and was about to call Jack when her cell rang. "Jill. What's happened?"

"Nothing. I've been sitting here waiting for you to check up on us again. You must have lost track of time."

"Blondie's here," Eve whispered. "I was about to call Jack."

"Can we give her a name other than Blondie, it's beginning to sound derogatory."

"Sorry, I can't engage my brain. Jack's got a lot to answer for. I haven't taken a single step without first looking over my shoulder. Two people stopped me this morning to ask about the murder. Everyone seems to know I found the body."

"How? I haven't said anything to anyone. Did you?"

Time to bite the bullet, Eve thought. "I might have mentioned it... in passing."

"Did you have an audience?"

"There's always an audience at the Chin Wag Café."

"Hey, do you think the murderer overheard you?"

Possibly. Yes.

But what difference would it make? She hadn't been

a witness to the actual act. "I've got to go. I have one more batch of cookies to do and then I can call it a day. I'll see you soon."

Looking up, she met Blondie's gaze.

Eve tried to act normal but found it difficult to do so when Blondie continued to stare at her.

She wasn't just staring. She was eyeballing her.

Again Eve considered calling Jack.

Blondie's eyebrows narrowed.

Recognition hit. Eve was sure of it.

Blondie lifted a finger and pointed it straight at Eve.

Who, me? Eve gestured by pointing a finger at herself.

Blondie nodded.

Eve shrugged.

Blondie moved around the counter and appeared to make a beeline for the door separating the front end of the bakery from the back. Luckily, the owner, Barbara, stopped her.

Eve watched Blondie gesturing toward her.

Barbara shrugged and shook her head.

This was getting out of hand. Eve held her breath and waited to see what Blondie would do.

When she swung on her feet and left, Eve strode out to the store.

"What was that all about?" she asked Barbara.

"That woman said she wanted to talk to you. She sounded angry. Do you know her?"

"No."

"Before that, she was asking about Jonathan."

Jonathan McNeil? The baker on vacation?

"She wanted to know how long he's been away. It's really strange. The police were asking about him too yesterday."

"What sort of questions?"

"They wanted to know if he had a violent temper. And..." Barbara drew her away from her customer's hearing and lowering her voice said, "They wanted to know about his private life."

"What about it?"

"You know. His tendencies."

"Tendencies?"

Barbara's eyebrows curved up. "His sexual orienta-tion or is it inclination?"

"Oh." Eve couldn't quite understand the signifi-cance. "And what did you say?"

"I told them I have no idea what he does in his private time."

"Was there anything unusual about him taking time off now?" it occurred to ask.

Barbara shook her head. "He always took time off at this time of the year."

Eve couldn't think of anything special about this time. Sure, the leaves were turning and the countryside looked prettier. Then again, she'd grown up in the concrete jungle so anything with color looked fantastic. "What does he do?"

"What do you mean?"

"Does he go away somewhere? Does he stay home to catch up with his reading?"

Barbara shrugged. "Whenever I ask what he plans to do he says he has a friend who comes in for a visit. An old school friend he likes to catch up with."

Could it be the murder victim?

"Does Jonathan live on the island?"

Barbara nodded. "Near the lighthouse. He has a small cabin his grandfather used as a fishing getaway."

Eve gazed out the front window. She couldn't see Blondie anywhere. Instinct told her to keep an eye out for her.

Despite her determination to stay right out of it, Eve thought she now probably knew as much as the police. What were they doing with the information? Keeping close tabs on Jonathan's cabin? Hunting down his old school friend...

"Why was that woman asking about you?" Barbara asked. "Are you in some sort of trouble?"

"Not that I know of. Maybe she's mistaken me for someone else. I should check the oven."

Eve finished the last batch of cookies and after checking the supplies for the next day she put in an order for what she estimated they'd need for the following week.

"All done for the day?" Timothy asked.

She nodded. Eve drew in a deep breath and smiled at the wonderful feeling of satisfaction she felt blooming inside her. "I've missed this. I'm looking forward to coming back tomorrow. I hope I didn't make a pest of myself asking so many questions about where everything is."

"It was fun showing you the ropes. You're easygoing."

"What's Jonathan like to work with?"

Timothy's lips tightened slightly. "He's good."

Eve smiled. "He has his bad days too? I've worked with those types."

"Yeah, sometimes... No one's perfect."

Interesting.

"But when he's good, he's very good."

Tell me more.

"He got me hooked on fishing."

"I had a boyfriend who loved fishing. Strangely, every time he came home from one of his trips he had a hangover."

Timothy laughed. "Yeah, that tends to happen."

"It's not much fun working alongside someone with a hangover."

She considered the small nod Timothy gave as confirmation that Jonathan liked to indulge and wasn't always the best company the next day.

Was he a passive or a violent drunk?

"I suppose everyone's different," Eve said. "I had an uncle who used to enjoy his drink but he never suffered from hangovers. However, after the third drink, he'd clear his throat. By the fifth drink, he'd be bellowing out a tune and wouldn't stop until he collapsed."

Timothy snorted. "It beats being a depressed drunk."

His eyes glazed over in a pensive sort of way. Eve imagined him thinking about Jonathan's off days.

"What are you getting up to for the rest of the day?" He looked like the type who'd enjoy a night out on the town. Tall, athletic looking, his thick brown hair had a tousled cut that never failed to look playful on a man.

He checked his watch. "Lunch with my friend. Then a round of golf. Early dinner and early to bed for my before the crack of dawn start here."

Not much of a life for someone his age. "Are you a local?"

"I live here but I'm not originally from the island."

"What brought you here?"

"This job opened up."

Someone with his talents and abilities could have his pick of jobs. Young people these days liked to balance work and pleasure. At his age, she would never have considered moving to such an isolated area with limited entertainment.

Jill had moved back to the island to recuperate from a bad experience working in the city and she'd since adjusted to the change of environment. It suited her to live here. Timothy's choice struck her as odd...

"You don't find it boring?"

He gave her a small smile. "There are benefits." Timothy shifted and again looked at his watch. "I should finish clearing up."

Eve felt he'd just given her a cue to stop asking questions. Annoyingly, the questions she wanted answered only occurred to her now.

Who were his friends? He'd said he was meeting a friend for lunch. Male or female? What were his sexual inclinations? Why had Jack and Mason wanted to know that about Jonathan McNeil? She decided to do better the next day.

"Have a good evening. I'm taking one of your walnut loaves home with me to try." With a wave, she took off, her attention on everyone she encountered. She only needed to cross the street to get to her car, but she took care to scan the length of the main street. If Blondie had decided to trail her, she'd be hovering around somewhere nearby.

Before she reached her car, she called Jill to let her know she was on her way. "Everything okay up your end?"

"I saw someone hovering nearby on the beach," Jill said, "But when I called Jack he said it was a police officer in civilian clothing."

Good boy, Jack, she thought.

"Also, Linda Brennan walked by a while ago."

"Was she alone?" Eve asked.

"No, she was with her walking buddy, Steffi Grant."

Steffi Grant, the woman Eve thought she'd recognized that day they were collecting signatures for the speed cameras outside the Chin Wag Café. Had Linda and Steffi been the couple she'd seen the day she'd gone to Abby's house and found the handcuffs? Being such serious walkers, they'd be in an ideal position to know who was getting up to what...

If someone wanted to have a clandestine affair they'd have to be very careful where they left their car.

Eve remembered the day she'd spotted them they'd been coming from the general direction of Abby's house. Surely they must have seen something... at some point?

Seen?

What if they'd actually done something? Had anyone bothered to ask them questions?

The thought distracted her all the way to Mira's house.

Chapter Eight

AT HOME, she prepared lunch and took it in to Mira who, according to Jill, hadn't come out of her writing cave all morning. Closing the door to Mira's study, Eve saw her absentmindedly reaching for a roast beef sandwich only to set it down and return to typing.

"I don't know how she does it," Eve said as she returned to kitchen. "Thank you for staying here, Jill. I felt much easier knowing someone was with Mira. How did you entertain yourself?"

Jill gave her an impish grin. "Mira works out some scenes out loud. It made for some interesting listening."

"Well, fun's over. We have to get to work."

"We do?"

Eve lowered her voice. "The police have been asking about sexual orientations. I've been assuming

Blondie is somehow tied in with the victim but what if... the lovers were gay?"

"Are they looking at anyone in particular? I've lived here most of my life and I've never met an openly gay person—"

Eve lifted a finger. "Aha. That's the key word. Openly."

"Who do they have in mind?"

"Jonathan."

"The baker? I'd never have guessed."

"We don't know for sure."

"But you're going to happily jump to conclusions because it'll tie in with a theory you're cooking up. And then we'll have our backs to the wall and be murdered in our sleep." Jill grabbed a handful of her hair and pulled. "What happened to you not getting involved?"

"I'm only playing around with ideas. Think of it as a game."

"A deadly game."

"Requiring pen and paper."

Jill sighed.

"The body was found in Abby's house." She drew a circle in the middle of the page. "Who had access to the house?" Eve tapped her chin. "When I spoke with Abby, I asked her about the house keys. There are only two. They... the lovers would need a key to get in." She went to work on a list and then pushed the page toward Jill.

"The realtor had a key. And everyone in the realtor's

office could have access to it. We need to find out names." Eve got her cell out and called Abby. She put the call on speakerphone and after a brief chat she got right down to it. "Lauren Wright." Eve circled the name and wrote realtor next to it. Then she frowned. "Hang on a sec, Abby." Eve went in search of the key to Abby's house. When she returned, she dangled it in front of Jill. "Abby?"

"Yes."

"When was the last time you had your locks changed?"

"Never."

"I figured as much. I've only now realized this is one of those old fashioned keys."

"Probably as old as the house," Abby agreed. "Actually, it is as old as the house. When I inherited it, I couldn't bear to change anything."

"So as far as you know there are only two keys. The one you had for everyday use and the one you kept in the bookstore and then gave to the realtor."

"Yes."

"You never made any other copies."

"No."

"Would your aunt have given a key to someone?"

"My aunt... My great aunt. I... I don't see why she would have."

"You said she never married."

"Are you suggesting she might have had a lover?"

"Do you mind if I play around with the theory?"

"No, why would I? Aunt Helene was a bit of a bohemian. I wouldn't be surprised if she'd had a string of lovers, but it's not something any of my family ever talked about."

"It wouldn't be." Eve drummed her fingers on the table. "We'll have to find out who was around in her time. You know, like a suitable lover and not necessarily an unmarried one."

Jill threw her hands up in the air. "That's nearly half the population. We'll have to look at town records."

"I have a box full of her personal things," Abby offered. "There are day journals, diaries and knick-knacks. Feel free to rummage."

"Okay. We'll report any findings. Bye for now."

Jill surged to her feet. "I take it we're going for a walk."

"How about a drive? It's a bit too far to do it on foot. I'll go check on the squad car and alert the police on the beach. As far as they know, we're going shopping. We shouldn't be gone too long. Whatever we find, we'll bring back here."

When they reached Abby's house, they both sat in the car staring at it.

Eve noticed the For Sale sign had been removed.

Pending investigations?

Abby hadn't mentioned anything about it.

"I guess they can't have people trudging about."

Jill agreed. "There'd be lots of curious people with no interest in buying the house but lots of curiosity about where the crime was committed. I'm surprised the police let you keep your key."

"Let's hope it's not an omission. I'd hate to lose my advantage. We should make the best of it while we can. Ready?"

"As I'll ever be."

"Remember, it's not the dead we have to be concerned about but rather the living."

"Yes, they always pose a real threat," Jill nodded, "Especially to people who go out of their way to make themselves a target. Remind me again why I agreed to come along?"

"Admit it, you're as curious as I am."

"I'm putting it down to my caring nature. If anything happened to you, I'd feel responsible."

Eve sent her gaze skating around the front of the house and got out of her car. "There's no one around. No squad cars that I can see. We're not doing anything illegal. I have Abby's permission to access her property."

"Are you talking to me or to anyone who might be listening?"

"Yes to both. And it takes my mind off ghosts."

Jill grabbed hold of her arm. "I'm not letting go."

"I was going to suggest you stay right behind me, but next to me is fine."

The house had taken on an eerie feeling. It felt too quiet. Quiet with an edge of trepidation. Almost as if the entire house had suddenly held its breath in anticipation of what would happen next.

At the foot of the stairs, Eve looked up. "Ready?"

"Yes, I have my running shoes on."

They made their way up to one of the rooms on the first floor where Abby had said she'd stored some of her aunt's boxes.

"I didn't like what I found the last time I opened a door. Here's to second time lucky." Eve eased the bedroom door opened and peered inside. "I never thought I'd feel so happy to see an empty bed."

"Now for the big test of courage," Jill offered. "Opening the closet door."

"There are only boxes in there."

"Right, then again, someone might have heard us coming in and they're right this minute hiding inside this particular closet."

"Thanks, Jill." The palms of her hands felt clammy. She wiped them against her sweater and before she could chicken out, she drew the closet door opened. "See, boxes. Actually, pretty hat boxes. I've only ever seen those in movies."

Jill yelped. "And spiders."

"Here, you carry these ones." She wiped the cobwebs off and handed them to Jill. A few of the hat boxes were empty, so she set those aside at the same time making a mental note to ask Abby what she planned on doing with them. They were certainly much too pretty to discard. In the back, she spotted what looked like an old trunk small enough to carry. She opened it.

"Wow. Packed full of letters. We've got our work cut out for us."

They loaded their hoard in the car and drove back to Mira's place.

"I'm surprised you didn't take another look at the crime scene."

"It's still fresh in my mind. Thanks very much."

As they drove back to Mira's house, Jill glanced over at the back seat. "Even if we don't find something, this is going to be fun. I always enjoyed history at school. It'll be exciting to get a glimpse into another era."

Eve nodded. "Who knows what we'll discover about Helene. I might start keeping a journal. Years from now, someone will stumble on them and read all about my adventures," Eve said as she parked the car. "How about we go in and have a cup of coffee to revitalize ourselves first."

They strode in, Eve carrying the heavier trunk while Jill followed with a couple of the hat boxes.

Hearing voices coming from the kitchen, Eve stopped abruptly.

She didn't recognize the male voice.

Gesturing to Jill to leave the hat boxes in the hallway, she set the trunk down.

"Hello," Eve said as she strolled into the kitchen. She glanced at Mira and recognized the police officer who'd been assigned to the beach. "Here we are, back again as promised."

"I asked Officer Matthews to join me for coffee," Mira said, "He ended up helping me sort out a character."

Officer Matthews smiled and gave a small shrug. "My sister's a big fan."

"Don't you think he'd make a wonderful pirate?" Mira asked.

"How are your sword fighting skills?"

"A bit rusty. My brothers and I grew up pretending we'd been shipwrecked on the island. I'm sure I can brush up my skills for Mira."

Eve brought out a plate and stacked some cookies on it.

"Oh, I was wondering where those were." Mira took the plate, held it out for Officer Matthews and then helped herself to a cookie. "Did you get your shopping done, Eve?"

Ah yes, her cover story. "No, I couldn't find what I wanted. It doesn't pay to be fastidious about the chocolate I use."

"You should suggest it to the store. They might bring it in for you."

"I'll do that next time. Jill, would you like a coffee?"

Jill seemed to be captivated by the police officer. "Um, yes... yes. Thanks. I'll help."

"I thought he'd never leave," Eve said.

"I'm sorry he did. Officer Matthews has very nice eyes. He seems easy-going but he doesn't say much."

"You might have had something to do with that. He couldn't take his eyes off you."

"I didn't notice."

"You were too busy looking at him. First chance you get, you should go out there and have a chat with him."

"I wouldn't know what to say."

"Ask him what he's getting up to on the weekend. If he's single, he'll likely tell you he's hanging out with his friends and that usually means the male variety." Eve washed the coffee mugs and dried her hands. Why would she assume it only meant the male variety? Timothy had said he was catching up with "my friend". She made a mental note to bait him into revealing more about "his" friend. The more she engaged him in conversation, the more chance she'd have of picking up a quirky trait. She hadn't noticed anything unusual in the way he expressed himself. These days, she knew gays couldn't be stereotyped and few displayed giveaway signs. "I'm trying to remember a line from a book... how does it go? You should leave him in no doubt of your interest or something along those lines."

"Pride and Prejudice. I thought you weren't well read."

"Mira has a copy on the coffee table. I read a few pages at a time until I finally finished it."

"Wow, that's two whole books you've read since you arrived."

"I haven't exactly been bitten by the reading bug, but I am getting better. Anyway, now we have the place to ourselves. Let's see what treasures we can unearth from these hat boxes." A couple of hours later Eve sat back. "There's a Henry mentioned several times but no surname."

"I've come across Henry too," Jill said, "It's all in reference to conversations."

Eve picked up another journal. "I must have the early entries. Helene talks about him as if from a distance. She describes the clothes he wears and his manner. Courteous. Good humored. Friendly."

"She talks about his garden in this one and how he invited her to cut flowers from it while he's away."

"Oh, I have a reference here to his return." Eve set the journal down. "I need thinking fuel. Coffee?"

Jill nodded.

While she waited for the kettle to boil, she tidied up

the kitchen and put some meat to marinade for their evening meal.

Glancing out the window, she saw a man approach Officer Matthews. They had a brief chat and then Officer Matthews left. His replacement, Eve guessed. When this was all over, and if Jill hadn't made any headway with Officer Matthews, she'd invite him over for afternoon tea as a thank you.

"I'm guessing they had something going on here," Jill said and strode in waving a journal. "Helene says she took a picnic basket over to Henry's and they spent the afternoon fishing. His conversation was lively and full of stories about his business endeavors in the city."

Eve clicked her fingers. "I get the feeling all that should mean something. It'll come to me. Here's your coffee."

They settled back down to reading and taking notes.

Eve shook her head. "Helene was one gregarious woman. Every day she called in on someone for a chat." Any one of her neighbors or friends could have had access to an extra key. How would they ever sift through the long list of names they'd compiled?

Jill sighed.

"What?"

"I guess we can cross Henry off the list."

"Why? Did he die?"

"No. He returned to the island... married."

Chapter Nine

ON THE WAY TO work the next day Eve remained on guard, still keeping an eye out for anyone paying too much attention to her. She made a point of going in early to town and wandering up and down the main street, making herself as visible as possible.

You want me, here I am, she thought.

It gave her the peace of mind she needed. No one would have any reason to go skulking around Mira's house.

Unlike the day before, time flew by and before she knew it, the day's baking had been taken care of.

Timothy had been busy showing a new baker the ropes. With Jonathan McNeil still away and the business never slowing down, Barbara had explained, they needed someone else on hand.

Once she had everything prepped and ready for the

next day, Eve packed up and headed home. The night before, she and Jill had made an inroad into Helene's journals and letters but had hit a dead end with the announcement of Henry's wedding. Eve hoped Jill had had more luck today.

Lost in her thoughts, she only got as far as unlocking her car when a hand clamped around her shoulder.

Startled, Eve swung around.

Blondie. Back again.

"I want a word with you."

Eve braced herself.

"You're not a tourist," Blondie growled.

"I don't know what you're talking about."

"The other day, at the marina. It was you pretending to be a tourist. You got me to hold your sunglasses."

"You must have me mistaken with someone else. Of course, I'm not a tourist. I live here."

"Why were you pretending?"

"You're clearly upset."

"Too right I am. You put the police onto me." Her mouth was set in a hard line. Her eyes looked as if they might pop out.

Eve tried to remain calm. "Hypothetically, let's say I did. If you have nothing to hide, then you have nothing to worry about."

"You keep sticking your nose where it doesn't belong, you'll get what's coming to you."

"Is that a threat?" Blondie had said it loudly enough

for passersby to hear and Eve noticed several people turn to watch.

Blondie jabbed a finger against her chest. "Stay away from me. You hear?"

"Loud and clear." She watched Blondie swing away and storm toward her car. When she drove off, she must have sunk her foot on the accelerator. The car disappeared in only a matter of seconds.

"What was that all about?" a woman asked her.

"Slight misunderstanding," Eve said, her voice shaking slightly.

"For a moment there, we thought we'd have to jump to your rescue," someone else said.

"Thank you." It was actually a good feeling to know she could rely on passers-by to assist her. She must have stood there for a good fifteen minutes trying to calm down. Possibly longer. She looked up and saw Barbara Lynch cross the street to her car and drive off. Eve checked her watch. It was close to lunchtime and Barbara sometimes went home for lunch. When Eve got in her car, Eve lost track of how long she sat there. Her hands shook and her mouth felt dry.

On the way home, she still felt so shaken from her confrontation with Blondie, she missed her turn into Mira's street. By the time she realized this, she pulled over the side of the road and gave herself a few more minutes to calm down.

She'd never in her life been involved in an argument

with a stranger, or anyone else. She hadn't known what the woman could be capable of. For all she knew, she might have been carrying a concealed weapon.

Feeling slightly better, she turned back.

Then half way to Mira's beach house, Eve heard police sirens.

They appeared to be headed her way.

When she saw them approaching in the opposite direction Eve's heart gave a hard thump against her chest.

She sat up straighter, her hands clenching the steering wheel.

"They'd better not be headed to Mira's place." She put her foot down on the accelerator, her teeth gritted. When she saw them drive past the turn-off to Mira's, she forced herself to slow down. Seconds later, they drove past her. She couldn't be sure, but she thought she saw Jack in one of the cars.

"This can't be good."

When she arrived at Mira's house, she found Jill on the front veranda.

"I heard the sirens. Are you okay?" Jill asked.

Just barely, Eve thought.

"What do you think that was about?"

"No idea. I guess we'll find out soon enough or not. I can't understand why the police are being so cagey. Why haven't they released the name of the victim?"

"We should organize a petition," Jill suggested.

"That's right, go ahead, have fun at my expense."

"I'm only trying to lighten the mood. You seem to be a bit on edge."

"I have good reason to be. You'll never guess what happened to me so I'll tell you."

They sat in the kitchen, Eve sipping from a tall glass of water.

Jill shook her head. "I can't believe Blondie confronted you. Talk about holding a grudge. She must have been simmering since the day before."

"The woman has a vile temper."

"Well, you did put the police onto her."

"That's no excuse. I'm a nervous wreck. I even missed my turn-off coming home."

Jill smiled. "Here's something to cheer you up. I'm going on a date with Josh."

"Who's Josh?"

"Officer Matthews."

"Fast work. How did that happen?"

"I did as you suggested and asked what he was getting up to on the weekend. He said he had no plans. I told him I was in the same boat so he asked if I wanted to catch up for a drink."

"A drink? Not dinner?"

"It's a start."

"I suppose if all goes well, you could suggest grabbing a bite to eat. Keep it nice and casual. No pressure."

"It's been ages since I went on a date. But now for

the big news." She held up one of the journals. "Henry's marriage was short lived. His wife ran off."

"That is good news. For us, at least. How did Helene feel?" Eve didn't think they'd find a straight out declaration of her feelings for Henry. She suspected something had happened between them, but they would have been discreet about it.

"She doesn't say. In fact, she stops mentioning Henry. There's a lot of stuff about his garden blooming."

"That could be a euphemism for her increasing interest in him."

"You'd think if something had happened, they would have married."

"Not if Henry remained legally tied to his first wife. Maybe that's the reason why Helene never married. I feel we're onto something here. But we still don't know who Henry is. I went to sleep thinking about it last night. Mira says she uses that trick to work out plot problems. When she wakes up in the morning, she finds the solution just comes to her."

"And did it work for you?" Jill asked.

"No. Maybe I need to practice." A movement outside caught her attention. Officer Matthews had come to stand by the back kitchen door. Eve stood up. "What do you think that's about?" A knock at the front door sent a shiver of apprehension up her spine. "Something's up. I can feel it."

She opened the door to Jack.

"Eve." He strode in, Detective Mason Lars a few steps behind him.

"Whatever you think I did, I didn't do because I was at work this morning."

"What time did you finish?" Jack asked.

"You're kidding me." He looked deadly serious. His brows had drawn down and his expression had taken on that deadpan look she'd come to recognize. Official. On duty. No-nonsense.

"Eleven o'clock."

"And you arrived fifteen minutes ago. It takes less than ten minutes to drive back from town. It's now one o'clock. Did you take the scenic drive home?"

"I... I had a run in with someone." She didn't want to own up to being at the receiving end of Blondie's wrath. Jack had already warned her about keeping her distance. Not that she would've been able to avoid Blondie. She'd been determined to confront her. "There were witnesses." And not a single one she could actually name but she'd recognize them if she saw them. Or would she? Eve had been so shaken by her experience she might actually struggle to describe those few people who'd commented on her run-in.

"Also, I stopped to chat with a couple of people." And that was the honest truth.

"Did you stop anywhere else on your way home?" Detective Mason Lars asked.

Her throat felt tight and the words she pushed out sounded strained and hard. "What's this about?"

Jack lifted an eyebrow to indicate she should just answer the question.

"I... I didn't exactly stop somewhere. Well, I sort of did. I missed the turn-off into Mira's street so I had to double back. I guess you could say I was taken off course."

"How far off course?" Mason Lars wanted to know.

"A couple of miles. I was distracted."

The detective folded his arms across his chest. "Where you anywhere near the lookout point?"

The lookout?

She'd been staying away from that part of the island. The last time she'd been there, she'd nearly been pushed off the edge. She tried to think of where she'd come to a stop. It had probably been near the lookout.

"I might have been."

"Did you happen to encounter Miriam Holloway?"

"Who's she?"

"She's the woman you approached at the marina and asked to hold your sunglasses. She says you came after her."

"Me? She's the one who threatened me. And... And I have witnesses to prove it. Right there in the middle of town. I thought she was going to hit me. She threatened me."

"When did that happen?"

"Today. After I left work. She ambushed me. That's why I was late coming home."

"Did you report it?"

She should have. "No."

"What did she say when she threatened you?"

"I can't remember the exact wording, something along the lines of me getting what I deserve if I didn't stop snooping around."

"You should know she's thinking of pressing charges," the detective warned her.

Her mouth gaped open.

"Why?"

"We won't know for sure until she's checked out at the hospital. She suffered a severe blow to the head."

"But she's otherwise all right?" Eve asked, her voice shaking.

"She was lucid enough to name you as her attacker." Detective Mason Lars slipped his hands inside his pockets. "Ms. Lloyd, would you like to revise your statement?"

"I didn't realize I had made a statement."

"Where were you between eleven this morning and one o'clock?"

Eve sunk down onto a chair. Had she spent an entire two hours trying to calm down after her altercation? It would be her word against Miriam Holloway's.

"At this stage we should advice you we saw you driving away from the lookout point."

Eve shook her head. "I didn't. I didn't do anything. I... I missed my turn-off. Miriam Holloway attacked me in town and I was upset." Eve knew she was rambling. She also knew she didn't have a leg to stand on. Surely her word had to count for something. "What was she doing at the lookout?"

"We haven't had a chance to ask her."

Eve held up a finger. "There's a path leading from there to Abby's house. It's not the most direct route, but it'll get you there. Maybe she's been keeping an eye out on the place."

"So you didn't lure her there."

"Why would I do that?" Outrage rose to her throat. "I'm trying to stay away from the woman. Now I have more reason than ever before. She's got it in for me. She knows I tricked her into holding my sunglasses and she's trying to get back at me for that. I, on the other hand, have no reason to justify attacking her. I'd have to be psychotic to do that." Her eyes danced between Jack and Mason Lars. "You can't seriously think I'd be capable of physical violence?"

Mason Lars gave a small shrug. "Maybe something she said triggered your dark side."

"And maybe you have nothing better to do with your time." She folded her arms. "I dare you to find a shred of solid evidence to prove I attacked Miriam Holloway."

"You sound angry."

If she didn't stop gritting her back teeth, she'd

ground them down. "You did that on purpose. Were you trying to incite me into violence?"

Jack was the first to loosen his hold on his straight face. "Eve. You really need to stay away from her. This only goes to prove it."

Chapter Ten

"THERE ARE plenty of entries for over a dozen Miriam Holloways online, but nothing on our Miriam. It's odd because most people have some sort of social media presence, even if they're not active."

"She's not going to make it easy for us." Eve raked her fingers through her hair. What role did Miriam play in the murder? Why did she want Eve to stop snooping around? Eve decided Miriam had only been angry about her meddling. She looked through the notes they'd compiled. Ideally, she would have liked to spread them out but she couldn't let Mira know what they were up to. Not that her aunt would disapprove, but she might worry about Eve putting herself in danger.

"Barbara at the bakery said Jonathan McNeil catches up with an old school friend who visits at this time of year. I'm new to the island, but you've been here longer.

Have you ever seen Miriam before?" Were Jonathan and Miriam lovers? No, that didn't make sense. Miriam wouldn't be old enough to have been a school friend.

"No. But I've never had reason to notice strangers."

Eve slid to the edge of her chair. "She's staying on a yacht. I wonder if there's some way of finding out if the yacht was here last year. The marina would keep a record but I doubt they'll hand over the information."

Jill gave a slow shake of her head. "Don't."

"Don't what?"

"Don't go to the marina. What if Miriam is out of hospital? Haven't you learned your lesson?"

"There's only one way to find out. I'll ring the hospital and ask about her condition." When she ended the call, Eve grabbed her car keys and cell. "We're in luck. They're keeping her in for another night. If I'm not back in an hour... call Jack."

Eve had no idea how to get the information she wanted about the yacht but she knew the opportunity would present itself.

"Why not just tell Jack about your suspicions?" Jill asked, "Let the police handle it."

"I'm not sure I'm talking to him. He was very underhanded yesterday. I didn't appreciate him making me think I was a suspect or that he'd think me capable of physical violence."

"You'd risk your life because of a grudge?"

"The moment I sense my life is in danger, I'll back

away. There's no reason for anyone at the marina to suspect me."

"None that you know of," Jill said under her breath. "I suppose there's no talking you out of it, so I'll sit tight and keep myself busy with Helene's journals."

At the marina, Eve strolled around the way a tourist would. Or even a local. As far as she knew, there were no laws against walking along the pier. She approached the marina office. The door was open but she didn't see anyone inside.

A computer sat on a metal desk. She had no reason to step inside the office, and she didn't think she'd be able to come up with one if someone caught her rifling through the desk. As for the computer...

It was most likely password protected.

Eve gave the office another cursory glance and continued along the pier.

No one stopped her.

Coming up to the yacht she'd seen Miriam Holloway head toward, she noted the name.

The Sea Fairy.

Compared to the ones at either side of it, it looked big.

"Hello."

She turned and saw a man emerge from a boat.

Eve waved.

"Are you looking for someone?" the man asked.

He looked to be about Eve's age. Same build as Jack

but not as good looking as him. "No, just having a look around. I'm new to the island and still finding my way. I've been here for a few months but only now thought of visiting this end of the island."

"I'm Rob Knightly."

Eve introduced herself, again thinking she wasn't doing anything wrong.

"This is a large boat," she said pointing to The Sea Fairy.

"It's a yacht."

"And what's the one next to it?" she asked trying to play it safe and show a general curiosity.

"That's a cabin cruiser, like mine."

"Do you take yours out into the open sea?"

"Sure, but I don't go too far."

"If you wanted to go far, which one would you need?"

"The Sea Fairy would do."

"I suppose it comes with all the perks to make the voyage comfortable. Any idea who the owner is?"

"Haven't met them personally and I haven't seen them around much. They keep to themselves."

Them?

"Husband and wife?"

He chuckled. "Maybe, I don't know."

He wasn't much help.

"I suppose you have people mooring here on and off."

"And then there are the regulars like me."

Eve looked away as if in deep thought. "So... a boat... sorry, a yacht like this comes in and docks for a while and then what?"

"Takes off for some other place. Down to Florida or the Caribbean. Some people keep to a regular schedule, cruising from one place to the other and then back again, like The Sea Fairy."

"So, it's been here before."

"I saw it last year. That's when I first came to live here."

Could she assume it had been the same time last year?

"I suppose those who can... do."

"Yeah, something like that. Nelson's back from lunch. If you want to know more, he'd be able to help you. He's the manager here," he said and pointed toward the marina office.

"Thanks." Eve didn't know how she'd wrangle the information out of Nelson but she couldn't go home empty handed. Once Miriam was released from hospital, Eve would have to keep her distance from the marina.

She wouldn't get another chance and she couldn't walk away with only a few snippets of information, she insisted. After the risk she'd taken, she needed something solid to go on with.

She wished she had Mira's imagination. Her aunt would be able to spin a tale convincing enough...

Eve smiled and strode back toward the marina office.

She stood by the door, again trying to look like a tourist. Catching Nelson's attention, she widened her smile. "Hi." She introduced herself and brimming with fake confidence, she told him a tale about her aunt sending her on a scouting trip. "Half the time I have no idea what she's talking about. She's a writer. You know, they live in their own world. Anyway, she wants me to do some research for her but I don't know anything about boats."

"What sort of information is your aunt after?"

"Well, she's writing a suspense thriller and the hero is a sort of modern day pirate. He goes from seaport to seaport, stealing from wealthy widows or something along those lines. My aunt's a stickler for facts, so she wants to know if yachts are likely to come in at the same time each year?"

"Why would she want to know that?"

Eve had hoped he wouldn't ask. "Your guess is as good as mine. I think she probably wants to give her hero some strange character trait where he's always sticking to a strict schedule, you know, like a personality disorder or fixation. I suggested he could be docking in the same place every year because it's his birthday and he likes to celebrate it in the same place. You know, because he's nostalgic. The thing is, my aunt likes to stick to reality as close as possible. So, while she makes up the stories, she wants them to have a hint of realism. So, her fictional characters have to behave in a way a normal person would."

Nelson brushed a hand across his chin. "There are a couple of yachts coming in every year. It's not unusual."

"Is *The Sea Fairy* one of them?"

"That's one of them, yes."

"And it comes in at the same time every year?"

He nodded. "Stays for a month and then leaves until the following year."

"Maybe he comes in for his birthday. Does the owner have parties onboard?"

"No. Gabe Stewart is a bit of a loner. He goes away for a month, then he comes back to his yacht and leaves. Although, this year he came with a girlfriend. She's been around a bit. Come to think of it, I haven't seen her today."

Girlfriend? Did Nelson have proof they were together? Had he seen them holding hands... or had he merely jumped to conclusions? "I wonder if she's the woman I had a chat with in town yesterday. She mentioned having a boat here. Her name was Miriam. She was lovely."

"That's the one, Miriam. Do you want me to tell her you came by?"

"Oh, no. Thanks. I'll call in on her some other time."

Eve had to force herself to stick to an easy stride.

Inside, she wanted to whoop with joy. Finally, she had a name.

Gabe Stewart.

He had to be the victim.

The police still hadn't released any details, not even the name of the victim, but it made sense. It had to be Gabe. He came to the island every year.

Nelson hadn't noticed him missing because he didn't expect to see Gabe Stewart for another month.

Now she had to find out where Gabe Stewart stayed on the island. And how did Miriam Holloway fit into the scheme of things? Was she a traveling companion? His girlfriend, happy to stay behind while Gabe got up to who knew what? Well, Eve had some sort of idea of what he got up. It had included handcuffs.

She was half way back to Mira's place when her mouth gaped open.

Could Gabe be the friend who came to visit Jonathan McNeil every year?

Time to find out where Jonathan McNeil lives, Eve thought. Barbara had mentioned his house was close to the lighthouse.

She was so lost in her thoughts she didn't pay any attention to the car driving toward her. It registered only as a blur. Her mental radar would have blipped only if it had been a black sports car. But it had been an SUV, like hers.

Checking her watch, she called Jill.

"Did you break the case?" Jill asked.

"I got some answers but they only lead to more questions. I thought I might drive down to the light-house and check out the houses in the area. See if I can spot the house Jonathan lives in. It's silly. I should wait until tomorrow and ask Barbara or Timothy. I'm sure he'd know. Or... silly me, we could check the phone directory. That should give us an address." Eve brushed her hand across her forehead. Her head was crammed with so much she hadn't been able to think of the simple solution until now... "How about you? Did you have any more luck with Helene's journals?"

"I think you're right about her using euphemisms. It's winter time and she goes on about how warm she feels and how she's never been so happy."

"No more mention of Henry?" Eve asked.

"No. It's as if he ceased to exist."

Eve tapped her steering wheel. Her thoughts wandered away...

Back to the SUV that had been going in the opposite direction.

Why would she think about it now? There hadn't been anything distinctive about it.

She mentally sifted through the vague memory and tried to reconstruct what she'd seen. She hadn't paid that much attention to the car. It had been a blur. Yet the image of the SUV driving by stilled in her mind. Like a snapshot frozen in place. She didn't know if she could trust her memory. The image she held in her mind could be any number of cars she'd seen that day, that week...

Yet in that split second, she'd seen something that had stuck.

The sunglasses.

Large... oversized sunglasses.

She'd seen them on a woman who'd come into the bakery.

"Are you all right?" Jill asked, "I thought I heard tires screeching."

"I forgot to check on something. I'm going back to the marina."

She didn't drive into the parking area. Instead, she stopped by the side of the road, her engine idling. From there she scanned the parking area for the car she'd seen, but before she could find it she saw the woman step off one of the boats.

The Sea Fairy.

The woman with the oversized sunglasses strode back along the pier carrying a small backpack and got in her car. When Eve saw the car moving, she ducked.

It took all her willpower to wait two minutes before following the black SUV all the way to the bridge that separated the island from the mainland. Once over it, it became easier to follow. Eve remained calm, even when she left enough distance for another car to merge in between them. Because of the height of the SUV, she could keep her eye on it without having to strain or stress.

As traffic became heavier, she took more care to stay close but not too close.

When the black SUV switched lanes, Eve stayed where she was. When she saw it indicating a turn, she again waited, taking her time to ease into the next lane.

Five minutes later, she saw the hospital in the distance.

"I can't risk it." She tried to argue with her voice of reason but the best argument she could come up with failed to convince her. Sure, she'd come all this way and it wouldn't kill her to be more daring, but she knew the woman with the sunglasses had come into the bakery and had been looking directly at her. She'd already had one run-in. She didn't want to incite another one.

Another piece of the puzzle, she thought.

The woman was somehow connected to Miriam Holloway and Gabe Stewart. She'd had access to The Sea Fairy. She knew Miriam well enough to take her a change of clothing. At least that's what Eve assumed was in the backpack.

Eve's heart thumped with wild expectation. She had to be onto something big here. If only she knew what.

Chapter Eleven

"I GIVE UP. What good is hindsight when it's slow in coming?" Eve crumbled and collapsed onto the table, her head just missing her plate of sunny side up eggs.

"Are you all right there, Eve?" Jill asked as she worked her way through her breakfast of bacon and eggs. "Give me a sign of life."

Eve lifted a finger.

"Now tell. What's on your mind? You know what they say, better out than in."

She struggled to sit upright. "Yesterday I should have gone back to the marina and..." she waved her hands in the air, "I don't know, I could have said I'd thought I'd seen... Gabe Stewart's wife... sister... or whoever... whatever that woman is, drive in and wondered if she was still around. The marina manager would have confirmed one or the other and I'd now know who the woman with the oversized sunglasses is. Instead, I'm thumping my head on the table. I wish people would stop cropping up in my life, at least the ones with murderous intentions."

Jill took a sip of her coffee. "So why didn't you go back to the marina?"

Eve brushed her hands across her face. For a long moment, she listened to her breathing. "It didn't occur to me at the time. I think I used up all my bright idea cards. Now it's too late and who knows, if I go back there, Miriam might already be back from the hospital and I know better than to poke that beast again."

Jill picked up her cell.

"What are you doing?"

"Taking action. I'm looking for the marina's phone number. You could call and ask if... Miriam is back and..." Jill's eyes danced around the room, "Oh... you could say you can't remember the name of the other woman, but if she's there, you might drop by..."

"It's worth a try."

"Here we go. I've dialed. The rest is up to you."

Eve cleared her throat. When the call was answered, she cringed. "Hi, Nelson. I spoke with you yesterday. I'd heard something happened to Miriam. Is she back at the yacht now?" Eve gave Jill a vigorous nod and a thumbs up. "She said she had someone looking after her... Oh, that's good. No... No need to tell her I called. I'll catch up with her later. Thanks."

Eve slumped back on her chair and smiled brightly.

"You're going to make me beg."

"No, I wouldn't do that to you. If not for your bright idea, I would've been kicking myself all day." She pumped the air in triumph. "It's Mrs. Stewart. Yes, that's right. The woman with the oversized sunglasses is Gabe Stewart's wife. Now his widow."

"Interesting. So, what's the significance?"

"Hang on a sec. I need to check something first." She dialed Jack's number. "Hello, Jack."

"You sound cheerful," Jack said.

"I have a question for you."

"Is it something I'll be able to answer with a clear conscience?"

"Did the police withhold the victim's name because they were trying to track down his wife?" She listened to the silence.

"How do you know about the wife?"

Again, she pumped the air. "Intuition and brain smarts."

"Otherwise referred to as a close encounter with the wife?" Jack asked.

"I'd seen her around and she came into the bakery. She spent some time looking at me. It tickled my curiosity." And now she wondered if she needed to add Mrs. Stewart to her list of people to be wary of.

"Did you go snooping around the marina again?"

"I'd never do that. Anyway, thanks. That's all I wanted to know."

"I feel used," Jack said.

"You'll live." She disconnected the call and tackled her breakfast with renewed enthusiasm. "The woman with the oversized sunglasses is Gabe Stewart's wife. I wonder how she feels about her husband's death? She didn't seem to be in mourning. In fact, she looked quite lively."

"Way to go Eve. You're back and raring to go," Jill laughed.

"You can't expect me to sit on this sort of information without doing something about it. Besides, Mrs. Stewart... now I'm kicking myself for not asking what her first name is... came into the bakery and I'm sure she was looking at me."

"Either that or you've become quite paranoid. I hope that's not a symptom of worse things to come. I'd hate to lose you to madness."

"Please try to be consistent, Jill. You were quite helpful before. You're either with me or against me."

"You can't blame me for trying to lighten the moment."

"I suppose." Eve finished her breakfast. "So, do we have Jonathan McNeil's address?"

"We sure do. We're lucky he's listed in the phone directory."

"Would you like to come with me?" Eve asked tentatively.

"I can't imagine what you hope to find there, but I wouldn't miss it for the world."

"Say it with less sarcasm and I might believe you." She gathered the breakfast dishes and washed up. "By the way, when are your parents coming back?"

"At this rate? Probably never. I always joke they'll go on one of their road trips and forget to come back." Jill stretched. "They called a few days ago to say they were extending their trip. Apparently, they met some really nice people and decided to head down to Florida. Mischief and Mr. Magoo seem quite happy here. I think they prefer your gourmet food to the kibble I feed them."

Hearing their names, they both lifted their heads and licked their lips.

"I'll have to cook them a treat for tonight."

"You don't want to spoil them too much. I might fall out of favor with them."

At work, Eve made an effort to engage Timothy in conversation but he kept his answers short. His weekend had been uneventful and the new baker seemed to be working out well enough for him to start looking for a place on the island.

"So, he's not just filling in for Jonathan?"

Timothy shrugged. "I don't know what Barbara plans to do. But she said we could do with the extra help."

At first, Eve didn't think too much about it, but then she remembered Barbara was first and foremost an accountant. She ran a tight ship and wouldn't squander money on an extra wage when she already had two bakers on the payroll.

"When's Jonathan due back?"

Timothy looked over her shoulder then lowered his voice. "He should have been back by now. He might be taking an extended vacation."

"So, you haven't seen him?"

Timothy shook his head. "He doesn't usually come into town. So, I'm not surprised."

As she finished up the day's baking, Barbara approached her. Her manner didn't seem as friendly as when Eve had first started working at the bakery.

"The new baker is happy to take over pastries and cookies. Just as well our agreement was on a day to day basis."

"So you don't want me to come in tomorrow?" Eve couldn't hide her surprise.

Barbara seemed to hesitate. "I hope you don't think I'm ungrateful. Your cookies were a big hit. Don't be surprised to hear from me in a couple of days begging you to come back."

It all seemed like short notice to Eve. Sure, they had been playing it by ear and Eve had been happy to take it one day at a time, but considering the success of her cookies, she'd expected to stay on longer. At least until Jonathan returned.

"I guess Jonathan is coming back then."

Barbara looked away and Eve wasn't sure, but she thought Barbara paled slightly.

"I can't say for sure. He was only having a short vacation and was supposed to have come back to work yesterday, but I haven't heard from him. It goes to show how unreliable he really is. Anyway, it's not a big problem. The new baker is working out really well."

Sounded like Jonathan McNeil was out of a job.

Strange that he should suddenly be labeled unreliable. Remembering Jill's suggestion that she was becoming paranoid, Eve shook the thought away.

"Well, it's been fun. Thanks for the opportunity, Barbara." She wasn't overly concerned about losing the job. Now she had no excuse to keep putting off her own business plans.

Although... Barbara's decision had seemed to come from out of nowhere. Had she done or said something to put her off?

Eve knew she should have let it go, but she needed to know.

"Was it something I said? I mean... you seemed to be happy with how everything was working out."

Barbara appeared impatient now. She'd probably hoped Eve would simply nod in acceptance and move on.

"The arrangement was only temporary. Besides, I think... I think you're more suited to running your own business. I know I couldn't possibly go to work for someone else now. Once you get a taste of running things your way, it's hard to adjust to taking orders from someone else."

Eve frowned. That hadn't been an issue. "Was there something I should have checked with you first?"

Barbara didn't answer straight away. Eve suspected she was fishing around for an excuse.

"Now that you mention it. Some of the ingredients you used were expensive. I work with tight margins. As it is, I had to put the prices up and customers don't like that."

She hadn't heard her complain before. Hadn't Barbara said the cookies were selling like hotcakes and she was taking orders for them?

"Okay, I was only curious." She didn't really want to make a fuss but it didn't stop her rising suspicions. Barbara had another reason for letting her go now. She had to. "I'll clean everything up and be on my way—"

"Don't worry about that. Timothy will take care of it."

Wow. Now she really was worried. She was being pushed out the door.

She tried to catch Timothy's attention but he made a point of looking away.

Coincidence?

On the way to her car, one of the customers stopped her.

"I hope I'm not too late to grab some of your cookies."

Savor them, Eve thought.

"You might just be on time."

The woman hurried off.

Eve thought about Mira's kitchen. It wouldn't be large enough for a commercial venture. On the other hand, the kitchen at Abby's place would be ideal...

She could have her own brand of cookies and sell them.

Eve looked up and down the main street. She didn't think Barbara would be open to stocking her goods and she knew the Chin Wag Café baked their own cakes and cookies.

"Shove it into the back-burner and get on with it, Eve." She had a house to look for. A business plan to work out. A man to track down.

"Jonathan McNeil, where are you?" She wished Jack would be more open about his investigation. Or... more absent minded, letting a few pertinent facts slip into their conversation. But he was always so guarded around her Eve thought he put in an extra effort.

Barbara had said she hadn't heard from Jonathan so she'd gone ahead and had employed another baker. It seemed rather rushed. What if Jonathan came back? He must have a contract. Barbara wouldn't be able to break it. She'd be out of pocket if she did and Eve didn't think the accountant would want to lose out.

"Expensive ingredients." Eve huffed out a breath. She'd been caught by surprise. Now reality began to sink in. She'd been fired. She'd never been fired in her life.

She'd been unceremoniously pushed out.

Something didn't feel right about it.

Eve would bet anything if she hadn't asked questions about Jonathan, she'd still be working at the bakery.

When she arrived home, Eve went straight upstairs to change out of her work clothes and into a pair of jeans and cable sweater.

"I thought I heard you come in," Jill said from the doorway.

Eve did the zipper up on her boots and looked up. "I got fired."

"What?"

"Barbara Lynch told me she no longer needed my services. She fired me."

"Oh."

"Is she on our suspects list?"

Jill visibly swallowed. "If she wasn't before she is now."

Eve nodded.

"Remind me never to cross you."

Chapter Twelve

"WHAT ARE YOU DOING?" Eve asked glancing at Jill who appeared to be counting with her fingers.

"Keep your eyes on the road, Eve. I'm doing a mental headcount of our suspects. I'm running out of fingers."

"Let's hear it."

"Miriam Holloway. Why does she want you to stop meddling? The first thought that comes to mind is that she's concerned about you getting in the way and messing with police work. But that's just me."

"What other reason would she have? Don't forget, she accused me of trying to kill her."

"That does raise a few questions. We know it wasn't you. Someone wants her out of the way too. We know she's connected to the murder victim. Maybe that's enough reason to hurt her. Miriam comes across as desperate to have you out of the way. Or... she might be so scared, she actually thought it was you. Someone hit her from the back and she has no reason to suspect anyone else. Or she could be colluding with the killer. They both planned the attack and pointed the finger at you. We always assume there's only one person involved. What if there are more? A conspiracy to kill Gabe Stewart. Think about it. Two people who could benefit by his death."

Miriam Holloway and Mrs. Stewart. "Our next suspect would have to be the person who actually ambushed Miriam," Eve reasoned. "Who could that be?" Mrs. Stewart.

"The real killer but that does away with my pet theory of there being two people in cahoots, Miriam and someone else. A theory I'm rather proud of. Unless I was right and it was nothing but a make believe attack. Then there's Mrs. Stewart. She was so helpful taking a change of clothes to the hospital for Miriam, but what do we know about her? Would she have solid motives for killing her husband? I'm thinking she's our wolf in sheep's clothing."

"We need to find out more about Mrs. Stewart," Eve said, "Do you think it's possible she and Miriam are in it together?"

"Possibly. You did say she didn't look like a recent

widow. Maybe because she knew all along her husband was dead."

"You're getting very good at this," Eve said.

"I've been reading a few mystery novels. Mira has a huge collection."

"I'd like to know what Miriam is to Gabe Stewart. Traveling companion? Girlfriend? Cook? The Sea Fairy is quite large. Gabe must have been wealthy enough to employ an onboard cook. And maybe Mrs. Stewart is one of those wives happy to look the other way."

"I'm curious. Why wasn't his wife with him?" Jill asked.

"Because... because this is his boy's only adventure so he sets off and leaves the wife behind. Or... she doesn't like yachting around the place. Some couples have separate interests and don't always do things together."

"Is that how it was with you and Alex?"

Eve nodded and tried not to think too much about him. They'd been married for several years and his embezzlement still came as a surprise.

"What else do we have?" Eve asked.

"Jonathan McNeil is now missing in action. According to you, he was expected back at work and hasn't shown up. Other than that, we have nothing else to go on with. And I'm surprised at you, Eve. I expected better. You should have been able to squeeze more information out of the other baker, Timothy."

"Sorry. I seem to be taking warnings to keep my nose out of people's business to heart."

"Jack obviously hasn't let anything slip, so we don't know if he's managed to discover anything more about Jonathan's sexual preferences... or whereabouts."

"Let's pretend Jonathan is gay, and... Let's assume he had a standing appointment with Gabe Stewart every year. Why would that be? Why only once a year?"

"They both have private lives. Or they're in the closet or so kinky, they only indulge in their *sexcapades* once a year," Jill laughed.

"That's not so far-fetched. They could have been each other's first lovers and even after all these years, they still keep in touch. Come to think of it, they might just be friends catching up once a year. Like a high school reunion. But then we have the murder victim and how he was found. I doubt Gabe Stewart was killing two birds with one stone, coming to the island to catch up with Jonathan and also meeting a lover." Eve knew they were going around in circles and pointing the finger of suspicion at everyone. But she couldn't stop scratching around.

"Do you think Jonathan could be the killer?" Jill asked, "Gabe Stewart might have said this was the last time and they could never meet again. Jonathan wouldn't accept it or even think he could live without ever seeing Gabe again, he decided to kill him and... himself, turning this into a crime of passion."

Eve gave a slow shake of her head. "If the police thought Jonathan had anything to do with the murder they would have put out... what do you call it? An APB."

Jill grinned. "That's an all points bulletin sent out to police officers. I looked it up. I think you're actually thinking about the police making a public statement."

"Yes, that's it. So why haven't they made it public?"

"Because unlike you, they don't like to make false accusations. They don't have enough evidence to pin the murder on Jonathan McNeil. Or maybe because they're trying to lure him out of hiding."

Eve nibbled on the tip of her thumb. "What about Lauren Wright, the realtor? We haven't even spoken about her. Or even seen her around town."

"She had a key so I think the police would have been quick to look into her. Obviously, they didn't find anything."

"There had to have been a third key," Eve insisted. "Do we have something to pin on Barbara Lynch? I'm still annoyed with her for firing me. And yes, I know how that sounds, but her being guilty would somehow make me feel better about being fired."

"Poor Eve. Okay, let's point the finger at Barbara. We know she took over the bakery from her father. Do we know anything about her private life? She's not married and I haven't ever seen her with someone."

"Here's something. What if, like Abby, Barbara

Lynch is desperate to land herself a husband? She sets her heart on Jonathan and starts an affair with him. He goes along with it because... he's trying to pretend he's straight. This is a small community and he's afraid of what people will say about him. I know it sounds dated, but let's run with it. Then, suspicious of what he's getting up to when he says he's going on vacation, Barbara finds out about his... Help me out, my mind's drawn a blank."

"She follows him to Abby's house," Jill suggested. "And when she realizes what's going on, she flies into a fit of rage and... I'm not sure she'd be capable of overpowering Jonathan. He's a solid looking man. Tall. Strong. What if Barbara had a gun and shot him? She disposed of the body and then she... she killed Gabe. He was already tied up. We don't know how he died. This is something else the police haven't released. Did you see any visible wounds, Eve?"

"No." She gave a fierce shake of her head and tried to think of something else before the image of the dead body filled her mind.

"No stab wounds. Gunshot wounds."

"No."

"He was tied up so she could have put a pillow over his face."

"Possibly."

Jill pulled out her cell. "Here's something.

According to this article, the skin around the nose and mouth of someone who's been asphyxiated may appear pale or white due to pressure. Does that ring a bell?"

"I looked but I didn't see. Meaning, I couldn't tear my eyes away, but I tried to avoid noticing details. It was gruesome. The dead body alone was too much information for me."

"So you didn't notice if the lips, gums and tongue showed bruising or lacerations."

"Jill, that's the sort of thing I'd notice if I performed an autopsy."

"Just checking."

"That's all right. You know, I rather like the idea of Barbara committing a crime of passion. Accountants always strike me as being dull. All that time spent with numbers." She shivered.

"What about Timothy Johnson? You said he was friendly at first and when you started asking too many questions, he clammed up."

"He too could be a jealous lover." Eve turned into a narrow lane. "This is it." She leaned over the steering wheel and looked at the house. Barbara had described it as a fishing cabin. Eve gasped. "Fishing."

"What about it?"

"Timothy said Jonathan had taught him to fish. Barbara said Jonathan had inherited his grandfather's fishing cabin." They looked at each other.

"Helene," they both said.

"Yes. Helene said she'd gone fishing with Henry. Could Henry be Jonathan's grandfather? If he and Helene had become lovers... then he would have had a key to Helene's house."

"And," Jill piped in, "Jonathan would have held on to it."

Eve slumped back on her seat. "Okay. Here's the problem. Why go to all the trouble of meeting in Abby's house? Jonathan had his own place. And, let's be honest, even if he'd found the key, how would he know which house it belonged to?" Eve shrugged. "It's a long shot, but maybe Henry kept a journal and actually named Helene as his lover. I know, it's more than a long shot. It's actually wishful thinking. Jonathan McNeil must have had a way of knowing the key belonged to Abby's aunt Helene and when the opportunity arose, he decided to use it."

They sat in silence, each one lost in her own thoughts. Then Jill spoke up.

"I'm actually okay with Henry having a journal too. So Jonathan knew all along about the key. When Abby put her house up for sale, he remembered about the key. And he and Gabe met at Abby's house because it was all part of a game. Boys like to pretend they're pirates. Jonathan had the key to Abby's house and he decided it would be fun to pretend they were meeting there."

"I like that." Eve turned the ignition key.

"Aren't we going to look around?"

"Yes, but I don't want to leave the car here for everyone to see. I'll drive down a bit and we can walk the rest of the way."

"Good thinking."

"We can access the beach from here." Eve climbed out of her car and stretched. "Next time remind me to bring some snacks. All this thinking has made me hungry."

The fishing cabin came into view. It turned out to be a small house, fit for one person. It sat at the end of a narrow street and only a few yards from the pier that had seen better days.

"See anything?" Jill asked as Eve tried to peer inside through a small window.

"Nothing. No one. Jonathan doesn't care much about personal comfort. He must be earning a decent wage. I would have torn this down and built something more comfortable and modern." They walked around it. "I can only see two rooms. A bedroom and a living area with a kitchen. That's probably the bathroom that's been added on," she said pointing to a part of the building that had obviously been a recent addition to the original structure.

"Meeting at Abby's house makes sense. Now if we can only confirm Jonathan is gay."

"Is? What if he was? What if something's happened to him?" Eve asked. "If it turns out the police know something's happened to him but are withholding the information until his next of kin can be notified, I'm going to be very angry with Jack."

"Why? Because you'd have done all this running around for nothing?"

"Exactly."

Jill's laughter was cut off when Eve clamped her hand over her mouth.

"I think I heard something. Or someone." She dropped her hand and gestured for Jill to crouch down.

They both looked at each other and nodded. Someone was definitely walking up to the house, the steps tentative rather than determined. Much the way someone would walk if they were looking over their shoulder to make sure no one was watching them.

They heard the front door to the house open. The slight creaking of the door suggesting someone was being very careful.

Eve bit her bottom lip. She desperately wanted to see who it was but if she tried to look through the window, she'd risk being seen. Signaling to Jill, Eve started moving toward the end of the house to position herself for a better view of the person when they came out.

Fingers crossed the person didn't head out down the beach, she thought.

It must have been twenty minutes later when the person came out. They heard the front door being locked which meant he or she had the key.

Jonathan? Eve mouthed.

Eve saw a shadow cross the front yard.

When she saw who it was, she pressed her hand against her mouth.

Her heart beat a fast tune against her chest.

She waited to make sure the car disappeared down the street and then turned to Jill.

"Well? Did you see anyone?"

Eve nodded. "You'll never believe it."

"Try me."

"Barbara Lynch. We must have been right about her having an affair with Jonathan."

"We need to tell the police what we saw."

Eve agreed. She didn't care how much trouble she got in with Jack. They needed to question Barbara and give serious thought to her possible involvement in the murder.

"She had a bag with her. Do you think she came to get some of her personal belongings, stuff that might link her to Jonathan?" Eve straightened. "I have a good mind to confront her. Now I'm more sure than ever she fired me because I was asking too many questions."

"But you won't go anywhere near her. Please promise me you won't. That could provoke her into doing something rash like getting rid of witnesses. If she didn't want you to ask questions about Jonathan, think how she'll feel about you seeing her coming here."

"You're right. I was just venting my rage. Come on, I want to call Jack and tell him our news."

Chapter Thirteen

JACK SAT for long minutes in silence.

Eve almost regretted telling him about seeing Barbara Lynch going into Jonathan's house.

What if it made him feel incompetent? He was a highly skilled and trained detective while she couldn't even pretend to be a hobby sleuth. If anything, she was an accidental sleuth. A sleuth by default. Eve couldn't escape the fact trouble seemed to follow her around.

It hadn't been her intention to outshine Jack. She tried to reason her way out of the sinking feeling by hoping Jack could think of their relationship as a partnership and not as a competition.

Please say something, she silently urged.

Jack surged to his feet and strode to the window.

She'd called him that morning and had asked him to

come for brunch or if he didn't have the time, coffee. Even police officers on duty had to stop for a meal.

Jill had been smart enough to make herself scarce by taking Mischief and Mr. Magoo out for a walk leaving Eve to tackle the subject by herself.

In hindsight, Eve wished Jill had remained behind to back her up.

"Are you naturally suspicious of everyone or is this a talent you've acquired since moving to the island?"

She didn't know if she should smile or scowl. "Are you going to question Barbara Lynch?"

"Of course we are. Thank you for sharing the information."

Now for the rest. He had to tell her off. To warn her, yet again, to not get involved in police matters.

Strangely, he didn't. Instead, he stepped out of the house and made a phone call. Presumably to Mason Lars to report Barbara Lynch's suspicious behavior.

"So, what's for brunch?" he asked when he came back inside. The edge of his eyes crinkled. His arms came around her waist and he drew her to him.

"Shouldn't you be rushing off to deal with Barbara Lynch?"

"It's all being taken care of."

Again, she waited for the reprimand she knew had to be coming her way.

"You look surprised."

"I'm... I'm bracing myself. Shouldn't you be issuing a warning?"

"Resistance is futile. I can't stop you from being in the wrong place at the wrong time. But I don't want you taking unnecessary risks."

"I won't. I promise. I don't think my heart can take it. Honestly, when I heard the footsteps heading toward the house, I prayed for the earth to swallow me. Well, I didn't exactly, but I did wish to be elsewhere. One confrontation in a week is enough to last me for a while." Eve swung away and busied herself in the kitchen preparing mini burgers with fries. "So... are you going to compare Barbara's fingerprints to the ones you found on the handcuffs?"

Jack chuckled.

"Right. As if you'd tell me. Although, I don't see what harm it would do. To be honest, I'm surprised Miriam's fingerprints didn't match." She looked up in time to see Jack shift slightly. What was that about? She'd gone to the trouble of procuring Miriam's finger-prints by getting her to hold her sunglasses. The police must have been able to lift the fingerprints off them and then... Surely, they'd taken Miriam Holloway's finger-prints. That had been the whole point of the exercise. She'd put herself at risk. Seeing Miriam free to wander around had led Eve to believe the prints hadn't matched. Had she been too quick to jump to conclusions?

"Jack, I get the feeling there's something you're not telling me."

"You know as much as you need to know or as I'm prepared to tell you."

"Which is nothing. You haven't shared any vital information with me."

"Information you need because..."

She gave an impatient shrug. "I'm not playing at being an amateur detective. The sooner this is over, the sooner I can get on with the business of... setting up my business, which has now been derailed by the fact a dead body was found in the house I hoped to convert into an inn."

"Is that what you plan on doing?"

"Yes. Jill suggested it and I like the idea. I've already decided I'm going to stick to cooking or at least incorporate cooking into my business."

"So, what's wrong with Abby's house?"

"It feels tainted. There'd be people staying there for the wrong reasons. You know, someone was murdered. I wouldn't want to become part of some ghoulish tour of inns with a macabre history."

"On the other hand," he said, "There's been one disaster. Chances are it'll be smooth sailing from now on."

"Lightning doesn't strike twice?"

"Something like that."

He had a point. "Would I be required to disclose the fact there's been a murder in the house?"

"It's already become public knowledge and anyone coming to the island would hear about it one way or the other."

True. It would only take a visit to a café and a brief mention of where the person was staying for the truth to come out.

"I'm still not convinced. People who stay in inns like to feel comfortable and... snug. While a murder might appeal to some, I doubt the average tourist would feel safe."

"What do you think they'll be afraid of? Ghosts?"

"Just because I haven't seen a ghost doesn't mean they don't exist. And what if I attract the wrong type of people? You know, the ones who think, well, there's been one killing here, let's see if we can have another one. I could become the ideal destination for killers. They'd be holding conventions at my inn." She shivered. "See, just thinking about it gives me the shivers and I'd have to work there day in, day out."

"You might feel differently after the dust settles. The house is off the market until we solve the case. So, you have some time to decide."

"Maybe. Or maybe some other property will come on the market."

He brushed his hand along her shoulder. "It's good to hear you talk about plans."

She smiled. They'd been playing it by ear, taking it one day at a time without putting pressure on each other. Eve felt commitment was something one arrived at by putting in the time to build something. A solid foundation.

"By the way, what's Mrs. Stewart's first name?"

"You never give up. Why do you want to know?"

"Jill and I like to toss around a few ideas." She shrugged. "Some people like doing crossword puzzles, we like to entertain ourselves with hypothetical scenarios. It makes it easier when we can refer to people by their first names. Although, sometimes we tag on the last name. It makes it less personal that way. At the end of the day, we still need to live with some of these people, even if they become temporary suspects. I don't see the harm in you telling me her first name."

"You're not going to like it."

"Please tell me it's not Mira."

"Eve."

"No."

"Yes. Eve Stewart."

"I suppose I'll have to learn to live with it. But please hurry up and find the killer."

"I'll do my best." He checked his watch. "Am I getting that brunch?"

"Of course. I'll get the burgers going."

After their meal, she brought out a couple of mugs and a plate for some brownies she'd made. "Has Eve Stewart been told to stay on the island?"

"No, she's waiting to organize the sale of the yacht."

She didn't waste any time, Eve thought. "So, you don't suspect her at all."

"She was miles away."

"You know that for sure?"

He nodded.

"What if she hired someone to kill her husband? She could be the mastermind."

"How's that chew bone tasting?"

"You can't blame me. It's all I can think about. Remember, I have a stake in this too. I found the victim. I've been confronted by one of the suspects."

"You can't help having found the victim, but the rest..."

"It's too late now." She helped herself to a brownie. "Burning question."

"About the weather? There's some rain forecasted."

"About the case, Jack. Don't be coy."

"I'm sorry, did I give you the impression you had access to police information? And don't say it's only fair."

"Hear me out. It might be something you could answer without breaching whatever secrecy code you have in place."

"Okay."

"It's about Miriam Holloway. Why was she traveling with Gabe Stewart? They obviously weren't lovers."

"What makes you so sure?"

Eve tried to remember if she'd mentioned her suspicions about Gabe's sexual orientation. It had been triggered by Barbara's mention of the police's interest in the subject. "I honest to goodness, cross my heart promise I didn't go trawling around for this information. It just landed on my lap."

"Go on."

"Barbara mentioned you asking her about Jonathan McNeil's private life. So, Jill and I have been playing around with the theory that Jonathan and Gabe were lovers." She watched for his reaction, but Jack had a perfect poker face. Although she thought she detected a slight lift of his brow.

"Ever thought of joining the police force? I think I'd rather have you on side than working as a private eye. You'd do me out of a job."

"Thank you. That's a lovely compliment. But no thanks. I don't deliberately go out looking for trouble. I simply don't have the stomach for it. It doesn't mean I'm not curious enough to want to find answers." Noticing he hadn't touched the brownies, she pushed the plate toward him. "I think you'll like these. They have chunks of walnuts in them."

He took a bite and sat back to savor it. Giving a

small nod, he smiled. "Are you trying to sweeten me up for more prodding into something you know could land you in a dangerous situation?"

"If I want to know something, I prefer to take the more direct approach." She took a sip of her coffee and counted to ten. "Do you suspect the killer acted out of jealousy? Jill and I think Jonathan McNeil had a full time lover and carried on behind her back with Gabe Stewart. That's right, I said her."

"I'd love to sit in on one of your brainstorming sessions with Jill. It would make great entertainment. What other theory have you been playing around with?"

"I haven't mentioned the obvious one. We think Barbara Lynch was involved with Jonathan. And..." She drummed her fingers on the table, "We think Jonathan is missing presumed dead because Barbara found him at Abby's and snuffed him out."

"Why? What was her motive?"

"She felt betrayed. She's in her early forties. I'm assuming she's never been married. Then here she is, running her own business, she meets the baker, falls for him or... maybe she sees him as her last chance to marry. He goes along because he's trying to keep up appearances or maybe just because he plays for both teams. It's been known to happen, but then she learns the truth about him and she can't take it. All she wants is a man to marry and she ends up getting the raw end of the deal." Eve was in full swing now, her voice getting angrier by the minute, playing the role to the hilt. "She hates that she has to settle for someone who can't even make up his mind about his sexuality. It enrages her."

Jack gave a small shake of his head. "It's such a wild assumption, it could actually be true."

Eve relaxed back into her chair. "Did you ever find out who the other fingerprints on the handcuffs belong to?"

"No."

He'd been too quick to answer. Again, Eve thought there was something not adding up. He'd said there were two sets of fingerprints. One belonged to her because she'd picked up the handcuff. The other had to belong to the killer.

"Are you going to get Barbara Lynch's fingerprints?"

"I waited until the coast was clear," Jill said as she strode in. "How was it? Did you tell him about us seeing Barbara going into the house?"

Eve nodded. "Confession is good for the soul. I think Jack and I have a new understanding. He definitely has a new appreciation of our combined talents."

"Our talents?"

"Did you think I'd take all the credit?"

"I'd prefer it if you did. Jack might forgive your

meddling because you're together, but he might not go so easy on me."

"On the contrary. Out of the two of us, he thinks you're the steady one. He trusts you to keep me in line." Eve folded her arms and pressed her chin down as if in deep thought.

"Is that a pensive look? Should I start retreating out of the room?"

"I'm thinking I might want to start looking around at houses. You know, for my inn."

Jill held her smile in place even as she asked, "Is this your way of getting your foot in the door with the realtor?"

"Possibly." She shrugged. "I might as well make the best of it and ask a few questions while I'm at it. I can't see any reason why we should dismiss Lauren Wright. She had easy access to the property. What if we're actually looking at a tryst gone wrong?"

"Whoa. Now you're weaving an epic fantasy. But... I'll play along. What if you're right?"

Chapter Fourteen

"A DISGUISE WOULD BE GOOD."

"What did you say?" Eve asked.

Jill brushed her hands along her thighs. "I'm thinking this is too close to home. I don't personally know Lauren Wright, but what if our paths were meant to cross at some point? What if one day I want to buy a house? Whatever happens in the next few minutes is going to stick. In her mind, I'm going to forever be the crazy person who walked into her office and accused her of murder. Not directly, mind you. But indirectly because I'll be standing right there next to you when you accuse her of killing Gabe Stewart, as you're bound to do."

"Feel better now?" Eve asked.

"Marginally."

"As far as Lauren Wright knows, I'm in the market

to buy a house. If our conversation happens to veer somewhere close to the murder case, then all the better."

She parked the car and checked her reflection in the mirror.

"I've never seen you do that before."

Eve didn't answer.

"Hey. You're nervous."

"I'm always slightly on edge when I plan to confront a possible killer."

"Could you wait until she gives us something to raise our suspicions before actually labeling her a would be killer?"

"Okay, I'll make that my new modus operandi. No more finger pointing until I have a gun aimed at me. Is that better?"

"It'll do."

They spent a few minutes outside the realtor's office looking at the listings. To Eve's surprise, there were a couple of houses on the island up for sale. Which only went to show she really needed to get out and about more.

"Can you actually afford any of these properties?"

"At a stretch. Although I don't think I'd be able to buy any of these houses outright. But I can do it without stressing. Besides, the house should be able to start paying for itself if not in the first year, then in the second."

"Sounds like you know what you're doing."

"You forget, I owned the restaurant. Not the building outright, but certainly the business. It had to pay for the overheads." She gave a small nod. "This will be better on many levels. I've lived in a postage stamp sized apartment in the city. The inn will be a different story. And I'm hoping, a better set up. I worked such long hours, it never bothered me that I lived in a tiny apartment, but now that I've been living at Mira's I'm thinking I might want some space. Come on, let's go in. And keep your eyes peeled for anyone looking and acting suspicious."

"I'll keep a lookout for furtive glances and anyone trying to make a quick getaway out the back door."

"That's the spirit."

Wright Realty had a nice ring to it, Eve thought. The reception area had a clean, no nonsense look about it. A couple of modern chairs in a corner with a real potted plant between them and a lovely painting of the seaside told her Lauren liked to keep everything nice and tidy.

"One of your paintings would look great here. I'll try and slip it into the conversation."

Jill groaned.

"What?"

"I had this sudden image in my mind of Lauren being carted away by the police and you calling out to her, by the way, I think it would be great to decorate your office with an original Jill Saunders painting."

"You mustn't jump to conclusions. She might be innocent."

Lauren Wright approached them. Dressed in a gray suit and pink blouse, she had an easy, friendly smile. She looked to be over thirty and wore her long honey blonde hair with the ease and confidence of a twenty year old. Eve couldn't help feeling slightly in awe of her and, if truth be told, she envied her on sight. She was the type of woman who struck her as always knowing what she wanted. Doubt didn't exist in her vocabulary.

"Hello, I'm Lauren Wright."

Eve introduced herself and Jill and told her she was thinking of setting up an inn on the island.

"I wish you'd come to see me a couple of weeks ago. I had the perfect property listed right by the beach. Natural light spilling into every room, a large country style kitchen—"

"Abby Larkin's house."

"Yes."

"So, it's off the market."

Lauren Wright lowered her voice. "You haven't heard? There was an incident." She waved her hand and flicked her hair back. "I do have another perfect house I think you'll love."

Eve tapped her chin. "I'd hoped to get a look at Abby's place. Is there any chance of that happening?"

"Not for a while."

"Did the police give you strict instructions to pull the house off the market?"

Lauren nodded. "But you can look at this other place today. I have the keys for that one."

Meaning she no longer had the keys for Abby's place.

"Out of curiosity, did anyone show any interest in Abby's place before it was taken off the market?"

"Only one person."

Eve waited for her to volunteer the information. Unfortunately, Lauren was determined to entice her interest in another property.

"I'm curious about the other interested party. I wouldn't want to miss out on this house. Just in case it comes back on the market and I happen to miss it."

"Oh, I doubt he'll come back."

"Why is that?"

Lauren Wright again lowered her voice. "Because it was the murder victim."

Gabe Stewart had wanted to buy the house...

Eve nudged Jill and exchanged a glance.

Had Gabe been serious about buying it? And what did he plan to do with it? Move in with Jonathan?

"I could take down your contact details. As it is, I'm a bit concerned about recent events. It might put some buyers off."

"Oh, that wouldn't worry me." Much. Trying to add credibility to her interest, Eve asked about the other house listed and decided the price put her out of the running. "Let me know about Abby's place. I'd be interested in having a look before it's listed again."

They left, Eve feeling the visit had been a waste of time.

On the way home, she thought about Jack's reaction or lack of reaction when she'd mentioned the second set of fingerprints on the handcuffs not matching Miriam's. "I think Jack is withholding evidence from me."

"How dare he," Jill said.

"Exactly. It makes my job that much harder."

"So now what?"

"Now I suggest we take a coffee and cake break. I'll have to figure out how I'll get Jack to tell me about his visit with Barbara Lynch."

At the Chin Wag Café, they chose a table by the window and placed their orders without making any more comments about their visit to the realtor.

Eve tried to switch off her thoughts by doing some people watching and Jill settled down to study the menu, which appeared to be new.

"Interesting that Gabe had planned to buy the house."

Jill flipped the menu over. "Yes. Interesting."

"I think The Mad Hatter's Teashop has changed their window display."

Jill looked out the window. "Yes. We should go take a look." She set the menu down and took a sip of water.

"I hear Willow Manning's dog had puppies. Are you still thinking of getting a dog?"

"No, I'm thinking about Gabe Stewart buying the house. I'm trying to think of something else, but it keeps hovering in my mind." Not caring she was sitting in the middle of a crowded café, Eve threw her hands up in the air.

Jill cupped her chin in her hand. "It makes me want to revisit our theory about Barbara being the woman scorned."

"Did we actually get around to sticking that label on her?" Eve asked.

"We would have, eventually," Jill reasoned.

"It makes me wonder if Lauren Wright told anyone else about Gabe's interest in the house. Maybe she dropped by the bakery to buy a cake because she wanted to celebrate the easy sale she could feel coming her way. One thing led to another and Lauren mentioned something about the buyer only coming to the island once a year."

Jill smiled. "And Barbara put two and two together."

"It would have been enough for her to become suspicious. I bet Jonathan never told her what he got up to during his vacation."

Jill frowned. "Did we ever actually establish... with absolute certainty that Barbara and Jonathan are... were... might have been an item?"

They looked at each other for a moment and then they both burst out laughing.

"Okay. So we both tend to get carried away," Eve said and wiped a tear from her eye.

"It would tie in nicely."

"Yes, it props up our theory nicely and opens the way for more suppositions. What if Barbara decided she too wanted to look at the house? Lauren showed it to her, Barbara spotted the handcuff the way I did, except she didn't say anything. That could have been the start of her suspicions."

"I think we've hit a dead end with that theory."

Later that afternoon, they piled Mischief and Mr. Magoo into the back seat of Eve's SUV and drove as close as they dared to Abby's place, getting out and walking the rest of the way to approach the house from the beach.

They encountered a few people out and about, including the walkers, Linda Brennan and Steffi Grant.

"You'd think with so many people about someone might have noticed someone who doesn't belong here hanging around."

Jill threw a stick and waited for Mischief to return it.

Eve hadn't realized how pretty the house looked from the beach. Maybe she could overlook the fact someone had been murdered in it. She'd be so busy setting up the business she might even stop thinking about ghosts and killers.

"I've decided I'll buy the house but only after the killer is caught. I wouldn't want them coming back to stay and gloat over how they got away with murder."

She glanced over at the nearby properties. Abby had said the owners lived on the mainland and used the houses only on weekends. Yet she could see someone working in a front yard. Or at least that's what it looked like to Eve at first. Now that she paid attention, she saw the woman bend down. She appeared to be searching the bushes—

"Is that Miriam?"

"Where?" Jill asked.

"The house next door. Crouching down by that pine tree."

"I think you're right. And it looks like she's searching for something."

"She's been hovering around the area enough to maybe... be looking for something she dropped."

Miriam looked up. Their gazes met and held.

Eve stood her ground but Miriam broke eye contact and beat a hasty retreat disappearing down the street.

"How can I not be suspicious of that sort of behavior?" Eve asked.

"I won't even suggest you try," Jill said and threw the stick for Mischief to fetch.

"Now I'm thinking the lookout is nearby."

"And that's significant because..."

"Because like us, Miriam might be leaving her car a

few streets away to avoid being seen. That day she was assaulted she might have been making her way here."

"So, the question that springs to mind is..."

"What is she looking for? Did she drop something when she made her getaway from..." Eve raked her fingers through her hair.

"Go on, say it. Abby's house."

"Why would she be in Abby's house? Why? When..."

"Ouch," Jill exclaimed. "I think I've been bitten by your bug. Miriam was in Abby's house, she dropped something there and now she's desperate to get it back. And, dare I say it, she was in the house because she is the killer."

Eve's gaze strayed to the house and a vivid flashback of the victim assaulted her. "I hate to think I went to all that trouble of getting Miriam to hold my sunglasses for nothing. Jack has a lot to answer for. Her prints should have matched."

"Only because you want it to tie in with your theory. You must feel inconvenienced."

"You've no idea." She gestured to the house. "It's perfect for me but it's going to take so much work to cleanse my mind of what I saw, I just don't think I can do it." She growled under her breath.

"You're scary when you do that."

Eve fisted her hands. "I need to do something. Take action."

"Oh, boy." Jill sunk her foot in the sand. "I wonder if I can dig a hole big enough to hide in?"

"Come on. Let's go home. I'm feeling hungry."

Eve couldn't let it go.

By dinnertime, she'd worked herself up into a frantic mess, with too many thoughts swirling in her mind.

"Miriam wants to get inside the house. We have to find a way to facilitate that for her."

"Send her an invitation."

Eve measured a few teaspoons of tea and poured boiling water into a teapot. "I wonder if she knows I have a key and if she doesn't, how can we let her know it's here for the taking? We could set a trap for her..."

"I thought I heard voices," Mira shuffled into the kitchen. "You two look as thick as thieves. What have you been getting up to?"

"Nothing," they answered in unison.

Chapter Fifteen

"BREAKFAST IN BED. Is this a practice run for your inn?"

"I'm trying to sweeten you up." Eve set the tray on the bedside table and drew the curtains.

"I'm still half asleep and I'm afraid I might be dreaming."

"Take a sip of coffee. That should wake you up."

"You're disgustingly perky for this time of morning." Jill looked at the clock on the bedside table and yelped. "Tell me that's not the time."

"Seven in the morning is late for me. Remember, I used to get up at four in the morning to hit the markets for the best produce."

"And my grandmother used to walk miles to get to school. Yes, I get it. But why am I sacrificing my sleep? Did you wake up with a spark of an idea?"

"Yes."

"I wish I hadn't asked."

"Eat up. Your eggs will get cold."

"Okay. I'm all ears."

"We need to scour through Abby's house. Go through every surface, nook and cranny with a fine tooth-comb."

"Right. Because the police obviously didn't do the job properly."

"I'm not calling them incompetent. But they're only human. They might have overlooked something. Miriam has to have dropped something there. She's desperate to find it and I aim to do just that."

Jill sighed. "That's a relief."

"It is?"

"Last night I worried you might be serious about setting a trap by spreading the rumor about you having a spare key to the house."

"I thought it was a brilliant idea, but I have to think of you and Mira. And I promised Jack I wouldn't take any unnecessary risks." Eve leaned against the window. "I think Miriam would have taken the bait. I'm sure it would have worked."

"But we'll never know."

"Unless we find what she's looking for. Then we'll have to make that public knowledge and set a crumb trail for her to follow."

"Sorry to rain on your parade, but what if we do find something? How do we prove it's Miriam's?"

"We'll figure it out when we get there, right after we celebrate finding something."

"At which point were you thinking of sharing the news with Jack?"

Eve lifted her shoulders. "He should have called me yesterday, but he didn't. For all I know, Barbara Lynch has been charged with Jonathan and Gabe's murder and we'll be wasting our time searching Abby's house."

"And you're too angry with Jack to call him."

"I'm going to start coming across as too needy. Why should I be the one to always call him?"

"Because it's all part of your civic duty."

"Yeah, yeah. Finish up. Shower and get dressed. I'll be waiting downstairs."

"Hang on. My date's on tonight. Can you promise me we won't end up arrested? I've been looking forward to this all week."

"I promise to have you back in time to spruce you up and give you some big sisterly advice."

Jill rolled her eyes.

After they finished their search, Eve decided they would open all the windows and let the place air out for a while. The air felt thick. She knew it probably had something to do with the tension crawling through her.

"The most obvious place to start our search is upstairs in the bedroom."

Jill's brows curved up. "You said that in one breath."

"I used it as my momentum," Eve said from the first floor landing. "It shouldn't be too bad. I have you with me."

"Like a lamb to the slaughter, I follow meekly."

They stopped outside the bedroom where Eve had found the body.

"No crime scene tape. I'm almost disappointed." Jill curled her fingers around the doorknob. "Ignorance is bliss. I'm not hounded by what you found inside, so it should be easier for me to open it."

"Thank you. You're a true friend."

"Please don't take advantage of the fact." Jill pushed the door open. They both stood at the threshold, their eyes skating from one end of the room to the other. "At this point, I'd love to say we came, we saw and we found nothing, so let's go. But you want to be thorough."

Eve crouched down on all fours and made her way toward the bed, her eyes scanning the floor as if looking for gold dust. "Keep an eye out for anything that glitters or... a piece of paper... or heaven knows, she could have dropped anything."

"It has to be something she might have dropped

outside too," Jill said, "So we can probably discount anything as insignificant as a strand of hair or an eyelash."

"When I was trying to cover my tracks about being here and seeing the handcuff on the floor, I told Jack and Detective Lars I thought I'd lost a bracelet."

"Something delicate enough to fall between the gaps on the floorboards?" Jill asked.

"Yes. Unfortunately, the gaps have been sealed."

"I would have thought that would be good. Imagine having to prod every gap on every board. We'd never get out of here." Jill peered behind the bed. "Any luck down there?"

Eve coughed. "I found some dust bunnies." She straightened and looked around.

"Help me shake the bed. Something might come loose."

"Good idea."

Rather than rattle it, they moved it gently and listened for anything dropping to the floor.

"Do you have a theory to go with this foraging expedition?" Jill asked.

"Other than suspecting Miriam of coming in here? No. I wouldn't even know where to begin."

"We could retrace our steps and run through the theory of killing Jonathan and doing away with Gabe Stewart."

Eve brushed back her hair. "When did we decide Jonathan McNeil was dead?"

"We didn't. It just sort of happened. Anyway, Miriam came in here and found her victim conveniently tied up. All she had to do was put a pillow over his head."

"And how did she happen to lose something?" Eve shook her head. "It would make sense if there had been a struggle. Maybe the victim grabbed hold of her ear and pulled hard enough to tear off her earring or a clump of hair."

"Not hair, remember you saw Miriam searching outside. She'd be mad to be looking for a strand of hair."

"Mad. Desperate. Same thing. And the more I think about it, the more certain I am about Miriam dropping something. She's been hanging around here for a while. Looking for her chance to get inside the house."

Jill hummed under her breath. "And she's right this minute making her way upstairs," her voice lowered, "A gun in hand because you forgot to lock the door behind you. Cue suspense music."

Eve jumped to her feet and swung around. "Why did you have to say that?" she whispered and inched her way to the door. Holding her breath, she peered out. She turned back and gestured for Jill to follow. "There's nothing here. We'll check downstairs, just to be on the safe side."

Jill might have been having a bit of fun, but now she had to wonder... Had she left the front door unlocked?

Had she even closed it behind her?

Eve had to fight the urge to bolt down the stairs. It had been stupid of her to leave the front door unlocked. She'd never been so careless in her life. She only hoped she didn't live to regret it.

Half way down the stairs, Eve stopped.

"What?" Jill whispered.

"I just thought of something."

"Your timing sucks."

"Where's a fire poker when you need one?" She wouldn't mind running into danger if they'd found something. But they hadn't. It wouldn't be fair...

They took a step and then both stopped again.

Eve looked up at Jill. Had she imagined hearing a floorboard creaking?

Jill gave a tight nod.

Yes. She'd heard it too.

When they reached the bottom landing, Jill grabbed hold of a handful of Eve's sweater. Whatever happened, they were in it together.

Eve had been so focused on taking one step at a time she'd been looking down to make sure she didn't trip.

Now she looked up.

Again, she tried to remember if she'd closed the front door.

It stood slightly ajar.

She couldn't remember.

She definitely hadn't locked it. It didn't register as something she would have done.

But had she even nudged it closed?

They could be worrying over nothing more than an oversight on her part.

Or...

Jill had been right. Miriam had been playing a waiting game, hoping Eve would return to the house so she could sneak in after her and look for whatever she'd dropped.

Eve signaled to the dining room on the right. She was sure that's where the sound had come from.

Her body buzzed with a surge of fight or flight adrenaline making it difficult to think clearly. In an ideal situation, she knew it would be better for them to split up, each one taking either end of the house. But nothing would compel her to suggest it. She couldn't push Jill into a dangerous corner.

It had been her idea to come here. It was now her responsibility to get them out safely.

They should cut their losses and make a run for it.

Eve pinned her gaze on the front door.

Reaching for Jill's hand, she gave it a firm tug.

But Jill didn't budge.

Had she been struck by a bout of paralyzing fear?

Reluctant to take her eyes off her target, Eve tugged again. This time, Jill tugged back.

"I found it," Jill said loudly enough to make Eve jump.

In that instant, she heard the scuffle of feet heading in their direction.

This time, Eve put all her effort into pulling Jill across the short distance to the front door. She didn't care what she'd found, she only wanted them both out of the house and running to safety before—

"Stop right there."

Or you'll shoot?

Miriam Holloway didn't speak the words, but the intention was there in the way she held the rifle pointed directly at her.

She'd actually brought a rifle with her?

Talk about being prepared.

"You can only shoot one of us," Eve squeaked and wished she'd cleared her throat first.

"That'll be enough for me. I think I'll shoot you. Your friend there is as pale as a ghost. Her legs are about to give way. I doubt she has it in her to run to the door."

"You don't have to do this," Jill said, "You'll never get away with it and you'll end up making everything worse for yourself."

Eve couldn't believe Jill had managed to speak. Her voice had been firm, determined. In command.

"It's too late to think of that," Miriam growled. "Now give it to me."

"You'll have to come and get it."

Miriam's lips tightened. She made a stiff gesture with the rifle.

Eve knew she wanted her to move away from Jill but nothing on this earth would compel her to obey.

She stood between Jill and the rifle and that's where she meant to stay.

Then again, her legs felt so stiff she doubted she'd be able to move an inch even if she wanted to.

Just as she should have been thinking of a way out of this mess, all that came to mind was asking Jill what she'd found.

What was worth killing someone over?

"Jill, give it to her," Eve murmured.

"No. If she wants it, she can come and get it."

It? It? What?

"It's not worth it, Jill."

"Oh, yes it is. I can't believe we nearly missed it."

"Shut up," Miriam shouted.

"It's your choice. And if you think about it, you don't have a hope in hell of getting away with this." Jill laughed. "There are two of us and that rifle is not loaded."

How did Jill know that?

"You want to test me?" Miriam took aim.

"At least tell us why you killed Gabe. It's only fair. You're going to kill us—"

"Kill Gabe? What the hell are you talking about?" Miriam shrieked.

"It's a bit late to pretend," Eve piped in.

"Why would I want to kill Gabe?"

"Oh, come on. You're not seriously going to plead ignorance. Look at you, all desperate and aiming a rifle at us." Again, Jill laughed.

Eve silently prayed she would tone it down a bit. She was still the largest and easiest target, but if given a choice, she'd rather not get shot.

"How did you manage to handcuff him first?" Jill asked.

"He asked me to."

What?

"I didn't want to do it, but it was part of his sick game."

Miriam's voice shook right along with her rifle.

Eve considered her options. She could lunge for it. With some luck, she might be able to get to Miriam before she fired. If she moved quickly enough, Miriam might lose her concentration.

Keep talking, she silently urged Jill.

"Were you guys playing some sort of kinky game?"

"Me? I wasn't. He was. I warned him. It didn't feel right."

The rifle lowered slightly.

Eve knew she had to act now.

Right now, she urged herself and before she could change her mind, she propelled herself forward.

"Drop the gun," someone shouted.

The command coincided with Eve landing awkwardly right on top of Miriam who struggled like a turtle flipped on its back. Her arms flailed, her legs kicked.

"Get off me," she shouted.

It took a few seconds for pain to register. As she'd pushed against Miriam, Miriam had reacted by lifting the rifle and the butt had hit Eve right on the chin.

"That's going to hurt and... bruise. How am I ever going to explain that to Mira?"

"Slide the gun over, nice and easy. Eve. Get off her."

Jack!

That had been Jack telling Miriam to drop the gun?

Eve twisted around and looked up.

Jack loomed over her. A police officer next to him held a gun aimed at Miriam.

Jill sat on the bottom step of the stairs, a hand on the railing as if she meant to get up.

"Hello, Jack." Eve managed a smile but only felt half her lips respond. Yes, it was going to hurt. Half her face felt numb. "We caught the killer."

Jack shook his head. "No, you didn't."

"What?"

He helped her up.

Chapter Sixteen

"WHAT DID Jack mean Miriam is not the killer? Can someone please catch me up?" Eve turned to Jill who was sipping a cup of coffee. "Where did you get that?"

"The nice police officer gave it to me." Jill smiled and looked over the rim of her cup at Josh Matthews who hovered nearby.

They'd both been escorted outside the house and now sat in the back of a squad car. Jack had told her to sit tight until the ambulance he'd insisted on calling arrived.

"Not the killer? Was Miriam Holloway even an accomplice?"

"Your lip is swollen," Jill remarked.

"Yours would be too if you'd been hit with the butt of a rifle. I hope I'm not drooling. I think I've lost all feeling on one side of my face. You'll tell me if I'm drooling, won't you?"

Jill put her arm around her. "Of course."

"And why are we sitting in a squad car? I'm suffocating in here." She jumped out of the car and leaned against it. "I hate this confusion." She looked down at Jill. "You did very well. You sounded so confident. How did you do that?"

Jill swung her legs out of the car but remained seated. "I've picked up a thing or two."

"Calling her bluff and saying the rifle wasn't loaded took some guts."

"A wild guess. I didn't think Abby would keep a loaded rifle in the house."

"Abby?"

"Yes. That was Abby's rifle," Jill said, "The one that had been hanging over the fireplace."

Eve frowned. She hadn't noticed. And she was supposed to be the one with the sharp observation skills.

"Miriam must have grabbed it when she heard us coming down the stairs."

"So..." Eve scratched her head. "When you said you'd found it, what did you find?"

"Nothing. I just went along with our theory she was looking for something."

"But... But... How could you have been so sure? And the risk..."

Jill laughed. "Now I know how a magician feels

about revealing secrets. All right. I was standing behind you and looked out the window. I saw the squad cars pulling up outside. I thought it would only be a matter of seconds before Jack or someone else burst in like the cavalry to the rescue. So, I figured I'd lure her out. It was a wild guess. We didn't know for sure there was someone in the house." She shrugged. "It worked."

"But we still don't know what she dropped."

"A charm from her bracelet." Jack strode up and looked at Eve's jaw. "How does it feel?"

"A charm?"

He nodded. "A fairy. Gabe Stewart gave it to her when she came to work for him on The Sea Fairy as his cook. It fell off. That night, it was her job to secure the handcuffs on Gabe." He looked away. "Here's the ambulance."

"I told you I'm all right."

"It won't hurt to make sure. You're going to have a whopper of a bruise. What if you have a fracture?" He lifted a finger and gave her a wordless I told you so.

"So how did you know to come here?"

Just then Detective Mason Lars pulled up in his car. When he opened the back door, Barbara Lynch emerged.

"What is Barbara doing here? I think I suffered a concussion. I'm more confused than ever."

"Why? You're the one who figured it all out," Jack said.

"I did? I feel I'm two steps behind everyone."

"We brought her here so she could walk us through what happened that night. We followed up on your sighting of her at the fishing cabin when she went to make sure she hadn't left any of her belongings behind."

It was Eve's turn to wag her finger. "You better start talking. If you keep this to yourself, I'll never forgive you."

"Can I do my job first?"

"All right. I'll be waiting at home. I'm warning you. You can't leave anything out."

"I need to clear the air. I didn't solve the case. Jill did. It was her theory." Eve gave Jill a thumbs up. "Barbara Lynch. Of all people..."

"Why do you sound surprised? You suspected her all along. You were right about her being in a relationship with Jonathan McNeil. And you were spot on about her catching him in the act." Jill pumped the air in triumph. "Go team Eve Lloyd."

"You seem to forget, it was you who linked Barbara to Jonathan. Did her fingerprints match the ones on the handcuffs?" Eve asked.

Jack nodded. He gestured with his phone. "News just came in. Jonathan McNeil's body washed up on the opposite side of the island."

They all sat for a moment in silence. For once, Eve didn't have anything to say. She hadn't known him, but she wanted to believe he hadn't set out to hurt anyone.

"Every time I asked you about the other set of prints, you were cagey," Eve eventually said.

"We found fingerprints belonging to three individuals, not two," Jack offered. "Yours, because you handled the handcuffs the night before Gabe used them for the last time. Miriam helped him put them on but her fingerprints were smudged. And then there was another set."

"Miriam helped Gabe put the handcuffs on?"

"She said it was all part of the games he played with Jonathan. He was supposed to come in and find Gabe all tied up," Jack explained.

"Oh." Kinky.

"And when Miriam realized she'd lost the charm," Jack continued, "She knew she had to get it back or else risk being linked to the murder."

"So, all this means I was also right about Jonathan's grandfather having a key to Abby's house because he'd had an affair with Abby's aunt, Helene." Eve's mouth gaped open in surprise. She looked at Jill. "We're actually quite good together."

"If you don't go into the business, you might want to consider writing murder mysteries," Jack suggested.

"Unfortunately, I don't have the talent for writing. All those hours sitting at the computer. It would do my head in. I don't know how Mira does it." She looked

175

down the hall at the study door that had remained shut all evening. "She's been at it all day."

"Don't you want to know the rest?" Jack asked.

"Oh, I thought you said I'd already figured it out."

"You did."

"Okay, I'll tell you what I think happened and you can fill in the gaps." She finished her coffee and sat up. "Jonathan had agreed to meet his lover, Gabe Stewart, for their kinky games. It was all part of his annual vacation. Some people dress up as their favorite comic book heroes and go to Comic-Con, others... live out their hidden desires and fantasies. Anyway, Jonathan had been having an affair with Barbara. He'd been leading a double life as a straight man during eleven months of the year. Barbara didn't like not knowing what he got up to." Eve frowned. "So Barbara killed Jonathan?"

"Barbara confronted him that night," Jack filled in. "She said she shot him and he staggered toward the beach."

Jill nodded. "We had this theory about Barbara surprising the lovers. We just didn't know how she got rid of Jonathan."

"Barbara Lynch. A woman scorned." Eve slumped back. "She must have been right out of her mind with rage. After shooting Jonathan she went upstairs and saw the proof of his betrayal with her own eyes. Am I right?"

Jack nodded. "She smothered him with the pillow."

"So how did her prints get on the handcuffs?" Jill asked.

"She walked us through it today. When she went up to the bedroom and found Gabe Stewart, she made sure the handcuffs were real and he couldn't move."

"Wow. That's cold blooded. I would have run for my life after shooting Jonathan. That could almost be forgiven as a crime of passion, but the rest... She must have been in a trance. Beyond reason." Eve thought about Barbara firing her when she'd started asking too many questions about Jonathan. All that time, she'd been working alongside the killer...

"I'm going to start keeping a journal. Honestly, when did we first suspect Barbara?"

The doorbell rang.

"That must be Josh. I hope he won't mind postponing our date," Jill said.

"He'll understand. We need to wrap this up." Eve smiled at Jack. "Thank you for sharing."

"You're welcome."

Eve drummed her fingers on the armrest. "So who attacked Miriam?"

"You tell me."

"Are you testing me?"

He nodded. "You must have a theory."

So, would Jill, but she was taking her time with Josh... "That was the day I'd had the confrontation with her. It took me a while to recover. I remember sitting in my car..."

"And?"

She lifted a finger. "Hang on." She'd been shaking and trying to pull herself together. "I saw Barbara Lynch leave and I thought she was heading home for lunch."

"She watched you having your confrontation with Miriam. She decided to follow her. Barbara was convinced Miriam had been involved in some sort of tryst with Gabe and Jonathan. She's not going to be able to plead temporary insanity. It's been days since she killed Gabe Stewart and possibly Jonathan McNeil and she's still angry about the whole situation."

"I suppose she feels hard done by," Eve offered. "I can't believe she was prepared to go on a killing rampage for a man who couldn't even be straight with her."

Jill and Josh appeared.

"What have I missed?" Jill asked.

"I just remembered something," Eve slid to the edge of the couch. "The day I discovered the body, I picked up a perfume scent in the bedroom. Next time, I need to remember to go around sniffing people. That might have saved me a lot of trouble."

Jack helped himself to a cookie. "What made you go to the house today?"

Eve and Jill exchanged a look. "We had a theory about Miriam going around searching for something. At first, I considered somehow letting her know I had the key to the house. Then I decided that would be too risky."

"So, you do sometimes listen to your common sense."

Eve smiled. "I have my moments. Anyhow, we decided we'd do a thorough search of the house, just in case your guys missed something. Then Jill joked about Miriam following us there. When we heard a noise, my first instinct was to get out of the house."

"Are you trying to impress me?"

"For future reference, I do my best to stay clear of trouble."

"Hello, are we having a party?" Mira asked as she strode into the sitting room.

"That's not such a bad idea. I could throw together some pizzas. Jill loves pizza and she deserves a prize."

"Oh, what did she do?" Mira patted Jill on the back.

"Um..."

"We found a missing piece of a puzzle," Eve said.

"Oh, I thought you might have solved the case you've been playing around with."

They all looked at Mira.

Mira laughed. "You're not the only one who can add two and two together, Eve. All that running around. Officer Matthews patrolling the beach. Not to mention the front-page news. I do read newspapers online. How many people did you suspect this time?"

Eve sighed. "Only the suspicious ones."

"You're improving." Mira rubbed her hands together. "Did I hear you say you were going to make pizza? I'm famished. Then, if you're all done wrapping up your case, you can help me play out a scene I've been having trouble with, Captain Jack Blackthorn has just met his twin brother..."